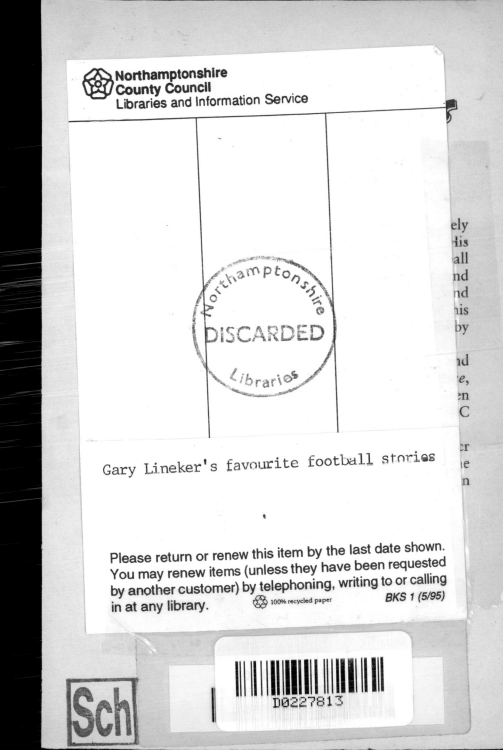

GARY LINEKER'S
FAVOURITE FOOTBALL STORIES

Gary Lineker is one of the best known and most widely acclaimed football players in the world today. His legendary career took him from Leicester City Football Club to Everton, Barcelona, Tottenham Hotspur and Japan's Nagoya Grampus 8, and he captained the England team from 1990 to 1992. His goal strike rate for his country placed him second only to the great Bobby Charlton on the all-time list.

He is now a regular and popular presenter on radio and television. He devised the screenplay for All in the Game, produced as a drama for ITV, and he has become even more widely known as a team captain in the popular BBC quiz show They Think it's All Over.

Among numerous other commendations, Gary Lineker received the Golden Boot Award for the top scorer of the 1986 World Cup, and was honoured with the OBE in 1992.

GARY LiNEKER'S

FAVOURITE FOOTBALL STORIES

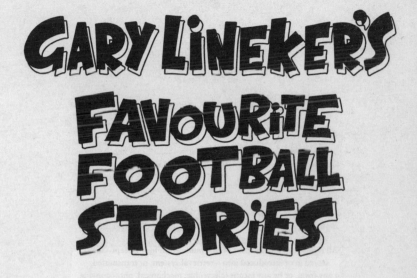

MACMILLAN CHILDREN'S BOOKS

First published 1997 by Macmillan Children's Books
This edition published 1998 by Macmillan Children's Books
a division of Macmillan Publishers Limited
25 Eccleston Place, London SW1W 9NF
and Basingstoke

Associated companies throughout the world

ISBN 0 330 35015 3

CONTENTS

Acknowledgements

The publishers are grateful for permission to include the following copyright material in this anthology:

Michael Hardcastle: 'Dog Bites Goalie' from *Dog Bites Goalie and Other Soccer Stories*. First published by Methuen Children's Books. Copyright © Michael Hardcastle 1993. Reprinted by permission of Reed Consumer Books Ltd.

George Layton: 'The Fib' from *The Fib and Other Stories*. First published by Addison Wesley Longman Ltd. Copyright © George Layton 1978. Reprinted by permission of Addison Wesley Longman Ltd.

Robert Westall: 'The Match' from *The Nightmare*. First published by Methuen Children's Books. Copyright © The Estate of Robert Westall 1995. Reprinted by permission of Reed Consumer Books Ltd.

Hi there, football fans!

Welcome to my collection of stunning soccer stories. I hope you'll agree that it's an unputdownable selection of the greatest football tales ever told – all that any football fanatic could possibly need for hours and hours of action-packed reading fun!

Here are stories of knife-edge matches lost and won; of moments of glory and despair; of friendships and rivalries on and off the pitch . . . In fact, all the drama and excitement of the world's best-loved sport!

I hope you'll enjoy the book. But don't forget – never stop aiming for the top. And never stop believing that dreams can come true. Sometimes they do!

Kev's Boots

Dave Ward

Kevin knew what they'd say the minute he pulled the boots from his bag.

'Look at the size of them!'

'Are you going diving?'

'Diving for penalties, more like!'

Kev shook his head. He knew he shouldn't have listened to his dad. When Kevin had told him he'd lost his boots, he'd hoped his dad might buy him a new pair, or at least suggest that he go over to his cousin's house to see if Steve would lend him his.

But no. His dad had said, 'You must be big enough to get into my lucky boots by now. I've still got them in the cupboard, you know. Leading scorer I was when I was your age, twenty years ago.'

Kev knew. His dad had told him a hundred times. But he'd never seen the boots before. His father lifted them down from the cupboard.

'There you go, son. Just need a bit of a dust and a clean. Rub in some Dubbin to soften them up.'

Kev pulled a face at the great heavy toe-caps. But it was too late to complain. He needed boots if he was going to play – and the match was that afternoon. They had to win it or Park End Juniors would be going down. But he knew just what they'd all say.

And he wasn't wrong.

'They look like diving boots, Kev.'

But Kev stuck it out. He was proud of his dad, even if he did go on a bit.

'Those boots have scored more goals than you'd ever dream of,' Skip, Park End's trainer, chipped in. 'And for Park End, too, twenty years ago. Let's hope they've not lost their touch – we could do with some goals this afternoon. I played with your dad, Kev,' he went on. 'I remember these boots. They scored some great goals. 'Course, I set most of them up. But your dad knocked them in.

'In fact, these must have been the ones he was wearing the last season he played. That final game was just like this afternoon – we needed to win or we'd be out of the League. He got one, too. Scored a cracking equalizer. But then there was a penalty, right at the end . . .'

'What happened, Skip?' the lads wanted to know. But Skip seemed as if he'd suddenly forgotten. He clapped his hands.

'Come on, lads. Let's straighten up. Kick-off in five minutes. Let's get out there. You don't need me to remind you – win this one and we stay up. But only a win will do. Anything else is no good. Lose or draw, and we go down.'

Kev finished fastening the laces of his dad's old boots. They might look big and clumsy, but inside they felt soft and smooth. Real class. He cast one last look around the changing room, damp and draughty on the corner of the park, then clattered out after the rest of his team.

Outside they were met by a sputtering cheer from a knot of shivering spectators. Kev smiled. He looked around for his dad. The applause sounded louder than usual, almost like a real match. In fact, Kev was sure he could hear a commentator's voice:

'They're coming out now. Just hear the crowd's roar. This is a crucial game for our lads. Only a win will do. Anything else is no good. Lose or draw and they're out of the League.'

Kev stopped a moment, puzzled. Where was the voice coming from? Then he realized. He was hearing the synchronized sound of a dozen radios. The usual crowd may have turned up to see them – mums and dads, uncles, family friends – but half their minds were somewhere else, because that afternoon Rovers, their local league team, were also playing a vital game. And just as for Park End Juniors, only a win would do. Lose or draw and they were finished. Out of the Football League.

At least Kev's dad wasn't glued to his radio like most of them. His mind was on the match, this match, here at Park End. He gave his son the thumbs-up sign, then gestured down to his boots.

Kev grinned. They fitted snugger than gloves and gripped the ground, sparsely grassed now at the end of the season. All Kevin could think about was that by that evening Park End would know – would they stay up or would they go down?

'Yes, will they stay up or will they go down? That's all this capacity crowd want to know.' The voice of the local radio commentator crackled around the ground.

Kev got a first practice touch of the ball. The boots seemed to leap for it – seemed to know what to do. He hit it spot-on.

"Not bad for a deep-sea diver, Kev,' muttered Bomber, the team's captain, as he ran past.

'You can feel the tension here as the teams line up. The captains shake hands and the ref flips the coin. And it looks like the home side have lost the toss. The teams are changing ends, which means Rovers won't

be kicking towards their own fans in what could prove
to be a crucial second half.'

Kev glanced at his dad again and touched the boots
for good luck, just the way his dad said he used to
do.

'It's been a season of ups and downs. The home side
started with a run of good results, but then their luck
didn't hold. As I said, a season of ups and downs.
One thing's for sure – they won't be going up. So now,
as the match gets underway, we just have to hope they
won't be going down.'

Kevin moved into his favourite inside-left position.
He liked playing there, just off the striker, ready for
any little tap-ins. He could hit it left-footed too, just
like his dad used to do.

The ball got stuck in the mud. A ruck of players
formed around it, hacking and kicking almost like a
rugby scrum. Kevin hung wide, waiting for the ball to
appear, trying to read the game, trying to see the
spaces, just like his dad had told him. And Skip too.
But he mainly listened to his dad – he had his voice
in his head when he was playing, going over tactics,
coaching him, praising him. Scolding him gently when
he did something daft.

But now half the time all he could hear were the
radios blaring out the big match news. You'd swear
Park End were playing at the Rovers' ground, not in
the park. He couldn't hear his dad's voice in his head.
Couldn't hear Skip yelling instructions. Couldn't hear
Bomber, though that didn't matter. Half the team
ignored Bomber anyway. Maybe that's why they were
down at the bottom. Maybe somebody else should
have been captain. Maybe Kevin.

But maybe that's what they were all thinking – that
secretly they all wanted to be captain. Maybe that's

why they never played as a team: too much self, never looking out for each other.

'Bronco, Rovers' captain, is on the ball. A controversial choice. He's not had the best of seasons. Some say he should stand down and make way for younger blood. He'll certainly stand down if Rovers go down. His job's on the line, and the manager's too.'

On the touchline Skip was shouting, knuckles clenched tight. He certainly only had his mind on one game.

'Bronco's lost it . . .'

And Bomber had too. He'd won it in the ruck and Kev was screaming for the pass – could see he was unmarked, could easily thread through, especially in his dad's boots. But Bomber didn't see him, didn't hear him. Maybe he was too busy trying to listen to the Rovers' match on the radios around the ground. Bomber's dad certainly was, down by the corner flag; he was hardly watching as his son, the Park End captain, clung on to the ball for far too long, got greedy, never even looked to see where Kevin was.

And Park End's opponents whipped it away. A maze of gold shirts, a lightning attack. They streamed forward, and Park End's goalie didn't even bother to dive as the ball cracked past him into the net.

'Now that's a disaster: Rovers one goal down and the match hardly started. Rovers' captain shakes his head and tries to lift his team. But some of them must feel that the goal wouldn't have happened if he hadn't tried to keep the ball himself for too long.'

Park End shambled back to face up. They'd been here before, too many times. Too many voices all shouting at each other. Kevin bit his lip, kept his mouth shut.

'Let your boots do the talking,' was what his dad

always said. Well, this time it was his dad's boots he was wearing. Kev wondered what they had to say.

He latched on to a pass and jinked upfield. The boots felt good. They might look heavy but they moved light as feathers. Almost as if they could fly – as if they knew the way. And they probably did. They'd been here before, on this very pitch. They'd probably glided over this exact same spot with his dad's feet inside them instead of his.

'And Rovers' inside-left's got the ball now. He's a tricky little player, ghosting his way through almost by instinct. He doesn't look up, just knows which way to go.'

Kev dropped a shoulder, dummied past his marker. Now there was only the full-back to beat. He was big. Looked almost too big for a junior team. He loomed towards Kevin.

Maybe he's clumsy. Maybe he's slow, Kev wondered hopefully, trying to remember what his dad always told him: 'Forget about the player, just think about the goal.'

The full-back's boots lunged in.

'A crucial tackle. Hard but clean. The inside-left is upended and gold shirts stream away upfield.'

Kev sat ruefully in the mud.

'Not so clumsy, not so slow,' he muttered to himself.

When the half-time whistle blew, Skip gathered the lads around him.

'Come on, boys, it's only one-nil. You've dug yourself out of worse holes before. Use Kevin a bit more – he's got his dad's boots on, don't forget. He was leading scorer twenty years ago – must be worth a goal or two today.'

The radios round the ground were tuned in to the

half-time mixture of jingles, analysis and news. But Kevin's dad wasn't listening. He was too busy thinking about this match. Thinking about Kevin out there playing. In *his* boots. The boots that had scored so many goals, here on this very ground.

The boots that could have led him on to stardom. Here, twenty years ago, at the last match of the season, he'd known there'd been a league scout watching from Rovers' youth squad. They might have signed him up. He might have got into the Rovers team. Turned pro. If only . . .

Kev's dad shook his head.

'The whistle blows. There's a tricky crosswind as this second half gets underway. One goal down, Rovers have to turn this around with everything to play for.'

Kevin let his dad's boots lead him on a diagonal run till he lost his marker, drifted free upfield.

'There's a neat move by the young inside-left. He's got acres of space. Bronco's on the ball. Has he seen him this time?'

'Bomber – up here!' Kevin screamed. This time his captain spotted him and launched a well-timed upfield punt. Kevin had to back-pedal slightly to collect it, but the boots seemed to expect that and gathered the ball easily, then picked up pace, cruising into space.

This time the full-back spotted the danger far too late, not expecting Kevin to switch wings. He lumbered across, but Kevin was through. Only the goalie to beat.

'Come on, Kevin! Come on, boots!' he could hear his dad yelling from the touchline.

'The crowd are roaring. He's through on goal.'

The boots glided on without slowing down. They seemed to have all the time in the world. Kevin didn't

7

even look at the keeper, just saw the goal as big as the side of a house.

And the next thing he knew, those boots were doing backflips he bet nobody did in his father's day. And all the team were hugging him, just as soon as they could get near.

'*It's in, it's level. Rovers have scored. But a draw's not good enough. They've got to press on. Got to put in one more vital goal.*'

Both teams tired as the game wore on. Play became scrappy. For Park End there was too much at stake to remember any of Skip's well-rehearsed moves. And even when they tried, their opponents snuffed them out straight away.

Kevin felt exhausted, but the boots didn't seem to notice: dragging him here, dragging him there. He had a few good touches, a few good runs, but the opposition had him marked now as a danger man. They weren't letting him through again.

'*Now, in the dying moments, Rovers mount one last attack. They've played their hearts out, they've levelled the score, but that's not enough. They need one more to win the game, to claim three points, to keep them in the League.*'

Kevin's dad looked at his watch. Saw the ref looking at *his* watch.

'*There's ninety minutes on the clock. It's nearly all over.*'

Kevin played a skilful one-two, slipped past his marker and gathered the return, heading forward determinedly, homing in on the goal. The full-back had seen him. He lunged in again, but this time not so skilfully. He mistimed the tackle, took Kevin's legs from under him.

Kevin lay bewildered on the ground, watching looming figures swimming round and round. The full-back stood there sheepishly, holding out a hand. Kev clambered slowly up. Still dazed, he realized that the ref was pointing to the penalty spot.

He half-expected one of his mates to make a smart remark about his 'diving boots', but he could tell by the lump on his leg that a penalty was the least he deserved.

'The drama here is boundless. Rovers have a last-minute penalty! If they score it's enough to keep them up. If they miss, it's curtains for them. Now who is going to take it? Rovers' history hangs on this kick. It's a big responsibility . . .'

Kev felt Bomber push him forward. He was about to refuse. He felt too groggy, too weak. But he knew they were all depending on him – and on his dad's lucky boots. Kevin looked over, but his dad looked away, hardly daring to watch.

Kevin's dad remembered only too vividly the last kick that he ever played on this very pitch. The crucial penalty that would have won the game, would have kept them up. But right at the very last moment, his lucky boots had let him down. They had seemed to stutter as he sliced the ball, and it had bounced back tamely off the upright.

Now here was history repeating itself. Another last-minute penalty in a crucial game. Kevin's dad was glad that his son only knew that the boots were lucky. He didn't know the luck had ever failed.

And if it hadn't, what would have happened then? Kev's dad always reckoned that the scout would have signed him. He'd have been in the Rovers' youth squad, might have made the team, turned professional. But then what? Years of travelling around the country, maybe even hitting the big league, signed to another team that might have taken him round the world. But there would have been no house on Park End Road. No Kevin's mum. His fingers touched his favourite picture of the children deep in his jacket pocket. No Karen and Billy. No Kevin.

With a strange churning feeling he wondered, if he *had* scored that goal twenty years ago, would he be standing here now, watching a boy called Kevin spotting up the ball and aiming to do what he had failed to do, wearing the very same boots.

'The young inside-left takes five paces back, runs up full of confidence, but then seems to stutter . . . I don't believe it, he's sliced it. The ball bounces tamely back off the upright.'

All around the Park End ground figures clustered round radio sets, faces filled with disbelief. Rovers could have rescued themselves, but now they were out of the League. Then attention turned back to the pitch as, almost like an action replay, Kev settled the ball on the spot.

'The Rovers team slump in dejection as eighty years of history go out the window. Rovers are out of the League. One kick was all that stood between glory and disaster, but the look on their manager's face says it all . . .'

Skip's face was set in concentration, not daring to shout, not daring to move, mouthing encouragement as Kevin paced back.

'Rovers' captain, Bronco, doesn't know what to do. He's trying to console his team-mates, but none of them want to know.'

Bomber wandered about the pitch, not wanting to watch, tugging nervously at his socks. Kevin stood still, stared straight at the goal, then bent down and touched his dad's boots for luck.

Kevin's dad flinched, remembering himself doing exactly the same thing just before he missed. But which mattered most, the boots or the kicker? Kevin's steady gaze didn't seem to flicker.

'The crowd are just standing numbly. They don't seem to want to go home. They don't seem to want to go anywhere.'

But for the crowd at the Park End ground, the agony still wasn't over. Kevin's dad wished he had two pairs of hands – one to block out the commentary that roared like an echoing nightmare of his own failed kick; and the other to cover his eyes as he watched Kevin run up, then seem to stutter as he reached the penalty spot.

The keeper's face was set like a rock. But Kevin didn't look. He saw beyond him into the goal, and beyond that again, his dad's face staring into space.

All around the Park End ground, disappointed Rovers fans held their breath as Kevin took aim with his dad's left boot, then threw their radios, hats and scarves high up into the air as they watched the ball swerve powerfully – straight into the back of the net!

Charlotte's Wanderers

John Goodwin

We met at PriceRite supermarket. I'd been working there some time stacking shelves on Thursday evenings after school. She was a new girl and I was given the job of showing her what to do on her first day. She wore the supermarket's green overalls, a plastic badge saying *Charlotte*, and a big smile which made her lips go all crinkly round the edges.

I'd never had a girlfriend before but I knew Charlotte was my number one choice. By week four of her shelf-stacking shifts I was ready.

'Do you ... er fancy ... watching a video?' I said, trying to make my voice sound real calm.

'What video?'

'Er ... *Vaults of Terror 2*?'

'Seen it.'

'*Braindead 3*.'

'I heard it was boring.'

'Oh,' I said, still trying to keep cool.

There was a pause. I looked up at her round the side of a stack of boxes of special-offer chocolate biscuits. She gave me a crinkly smile.

'Laurel and Hardy?' she said.

'Yeah!'

'Really?'

'Why not?'

It was agreed we would meet at her house on

Saturday for a session of video viewing. I did wheelies up and down the pavements all the way home that Thursday evening, not minding a bit that I really hated Laurel and Hardy. The countdown to my first serious date had already begun and there were only 2,580 minutes to go until Saturday at three o'clock.

We had a whole month of video watching. Four glorious weeks of zombie terror and Laurel and Hardy. In the fifth week I went up to her house as usual. Her dad opened the door and said she was out.

'Didn't you know?' he said. 'She's gone to football.'

'Gone to football?' I repeated.

'Yes.'

I opened and closed my mouth in silence like a demented zombie from the video we wouldn't be watching. Her dad started to close the door and I knew I had to find something else to say to him to try and make sense of what was happening.

'I didn't know she liked watching football,' I said. Her dad gave me a hard look.

'You've got it wrong,' he said. 'She isn't *watching* football, she's playing it. Down on Park Grove.'

With that he was gone and the door was closed. I walked down their drive and sat on my bike. Charlotte was *playing football*. Why hadn't she told me about it?

I looked back towards their house, hoping that Charlotte would suddenly open the door and come running out saying it was only a joke. Only she didn't. The house looked still and empty.

I peered down at my handlebars. They were pointing in the direction of Park Grove. It would be a long cycle, ten miles at least, and most of it uphill. But if I started now I could be there before the game was finished. Maybe see a fair bit of the second half if I pedalled hard.

Then I was off. Down Packer Lane, onto the cinder track, over the railway bridge and out onto the main road and making good time. Round the big round-about and into ... I stopped. Pulled my brakes on hard. Of course. I was so stupid. Really thick. Charlotte wasn't playing football down Park Grove. No way. Not her. It was the push-off. An excuse. She'd had enough of me. Fed up with Saturday video watching and she hadn't the guts to tell me herself. She'd got her dad to do the dirty work for her. I turned the bike round and slowly, very slowly, made my way back home.

I dreaded Thursday. I thought of not going to work. Perhaps I could phone in saying I'd got the flu. But I needed the money – with Christmas coming along there were loads of presents to buy. Still, there was one big present I didn't have to worry about any longer.

I saw her straight away, coming out of the stockroom. She came towards me.

'We need to talk,' she said and tugged the sleeve of my overall, starting to pull me back towards the stockroom. Only Mrs Hillett came along and saw us and pointed towards 'Confectionery and Household'. When Mrs Hillett points her skinny finger you move – if you want to keep your job that is.

It was finishing time before we had a chance to meet. Charlotte waited for me in the car park.

'Sorry about Saturday,' she said.

'I thought we were finished,' I said.

'Of course not ... I just didn't have a chance to tell you. It all happened so fast. The team were short of a player and I couldn't let them down. I tried to phone.'

A rusty old van with its front bumper tied on with rope pulled into the car park and started to honk its horn.

'That's Marie . . . I've got to go. It's training tonight.'

'But . . .'

Charlotte waved in the direction of the van.

'I'd better go,' she said. Then she kissed me and ran off. Just before she got to the van she turned and shouted.

'Come on Saturday. To the match. It's at Park Grove . . . three o'clock kick-off.'

I could taste her kiss for days. It lured me on like a magnet to Park Grove. I decided I didn't want to appear too keen, too desperate to see her, so I got there at half-time.

The teams were in huddles at opposite ends of the pitch sucking bits of orange. One huddle was in a blue strip, the other in yellow and black. I searched both huddles for the head of ginger hair and crinkly smile that belonged to Charlotte. She was in the middle of the blue shirts, only she wasn't smiling but listening very hard to a thin woman who was giving them all some grief. I could see this must be Marie from the rusty van. They were obviously losing.

Then a whistle went, Marie collected in the bits of leftover oranges and the two teams changed ends ready to begin the second half.

The next forty-five minutes were a disaster. Marie ran up and down the touchline just like my dad used to when I played in the junior school football team, only Marie ran faster and shouted louder. In fact much louder. It all came out in a garbled gabble like a never-ending stream:

'Kik it tout. Kik it tout. Tout tout tout. CrossitEllen. CrossitEllen. StopitJo. Passitpassit. Upup. Up pup pup. ChaseitLin. Chaseit. Kikittoutkikittouttouttouttout.'

She didn't stop for forty-five minutes. It made my head hurt listening to her.

All her shouting and running were a waste of time. They lost three-nil. The more she shouted the worse they played. The backs were forward when they should have been back, and the forwards were back when they should have been forward. The goalie let in the softest goal by looking at Marie when she should have been looking at the ball. In the last ten minutes of the match they truly lived up to their names of 'The Women's Wanderers' by wandering about all over the pitch without any sense of purpose or direction.

As the final whistle blew and all the players started to leave the pitch I wondered if it was best for me to slip away quietly on my bike and head for home. But my feet were rooted to the ground and I couldn't move. Charlotte looked at me for the first time that afternoon and shook her head. I reckoned she was ready to burst into tears. Then Marie gathered them all up in another huddle and I knew it was time to climb onto my saddle and head off home.

I was woken early the next morning. Somebody was knocking on our back door. The somebody was Charlotte, still dressed in her football gear. I went down to let her in.

'Marie says we should have extra practice. I thought you'd help me.'

'But it's half past eight on a Sunday morning!'

'So?'

We went down to a bit of waste ground by the scrapyard and began to kick a ball about.

'We've got to work . . . at the . . . midfield linkage,' said Charlotte between kicks. 'Not getting caught . . . in the . . . offside trap . . . that's what Marie tells us . . . in her team talk.'

I trapped the ball hard with my foot.

'Talk is OK,' I said. 'But . . .'

'But what?'

I spun round with the ball at my feet. Charlotte started to kick at my ankles, trying to hit the ball away.

'Talk is OK,' I repeated, 'but it's skill that counts.' She lashed out with her foot, barged me with her shoulder and as I fell to the ground she grabbed the ball with her hands.

'Like that skill?' she shouted and began to hit me with the ball. 'You think we're crap, don't you? Mr Clever Boots . . . Think just because we're a women's team we can't play decent football.'

She was hitting me harder and harder with the ball.

'You men . . . think you know it all . . . We'll show you . . .'

I took the ball from her and said quietly, 'I was just trying to say . . .'

'Well, don't.'

She grabbed the ball again and ran off to kick it angrily against the wire fence of the scrapyard. I picked myself up from the ground and watched her, pleased I wasn't the wire fence. I'd had enough dents and bashes for one Sunday morning.

When her anger had started to die down a bit I went over.

'What about heading?'

She just carried on kicking and ignored me.

'How's your heading?' I said.

'It's fine . . . It's just you who's doing my head in . . .

all you men . . .' she said and kicked the ball viciously at me.

Her heading was poor. In fact she couldn't head the ball at all, but I didn't make any comment about it. Every time I threw the ball in the air she ran to head it and then pulled away at the last minute and missed it by a mile. Then I remembered an old tactic my dad used to try.

'Jump' I said.

'What?'

'Jump in the air as high as you can.'

'But we're supposed to be trying heading.'

'Yeah . . . and it's all part of it . . . to build confidence. Jump on the spot as high as you can. Come on – go for it.'

For the next ten minutes we jumped about like two crazed kangaroos till we could jump no more. Then I took hold of the ball and held it up to her forehead.

'Knock it out of my hands.'

'What?'

'Just do it.'

After three goes I held the ball further from her forehead and we repeated the exercise. Each time she hit the ball hard and true with her forehead. Then I began to throw the ball very gently in the air and again she hit it true. I threw it higher.

'Head through the ball . . . through it.' And so she did.

'Now we'll put the two together . . . I'm going to throw it really high . . . You leap in the air and head it . . . Right?'

'Right.'

I threw, she leapt, the ball missed her head and hit her smack on her nose. She fell to the ground and blood trickled out of her nose, down her face and onto her shirt. I ran over in a panic towards her. Down on the floor her face was screwed up in pain.

'Charlotte . . . are you all right?' I cried.

She looked up at me and her face broke into a smile. She got up and began to wipe away the blood from her face and shirt. I wanted us to take a break and go back home for a bit of easy TV cartoon watching but she was having none of it.

'No,' she said. 'I'm going to get this sorted.'

And sorted it was. I threw the ball high, she hit it in the middle of her forehead and the ball sailed up in the air over the wire fence and into the scrapyard.

'One-nil,' she shouted. 'One-bloomin'-nil.' And she jumped higher in the air than any kangaroo or Man U player ever has. I looked at her in a gob-smacked sort of way.

'Now we're ready,' she said. 'Ready for our next match.'

The next match was different. For a start there was no Marie hurtling down the touchline shouting abuse at twenty zillion decibels. Apparently she'd had to go away on business up north. I reckoned she'd given up on The Women's Wanderers and gone to give some other poor team the benefit of her 90-minute verbal abuse and touchline torment.

There was a thick fog as the teams kicked off, and total silence. I strained my eyes and ears to be sure there really were twenty-two players out there and that they hadn't cleared off to the changing rooms to leave me standing alone like a lonely lemon. The occasional sound of the ref's whistle and lurching ghostly grey half-figures appearing and then dis-appearing in and out of the fog were the sum total of my impressions of the first half.

At half-time the two teams didn't dare stand too far

apart in their orange-sucking huddles in case they never found each other again. There was talk of abandoning the game. It seemed as if all our Sunday-morning, blood-bursting, head-throbbing efforts down by the scrapyard were in vain. The ref had her head in the rule book trying to work out what to do in the event of a fog-logged game, when the fog started to thin under the heat of a feeble December sun. Strands of the fog swirled about and began to drift off in the direction of both goals, leaving the middle of the pitch in clear air. The match was saved and the second half began.

Most of the early play was in the Wanderers' half with a gaggle of players all scrabbling about near the goalmouth. At least I *think* it was a gaggle playing football and not doing a spot of disco dancing – the fog was still pretty thick around that part of the pitch. Then there was a shout, a whistle, a cheer and the Wanderers were one-nil down.

Straight from the kick-off the play switched to the opposition's goalmouth with a repeat of the disco dancing impressions. I ran down the touchline to get a closer look and was just near enough to see the ball skid off an opposition boot for a Wanderers' corner. I ran round behind the goal as the corner kick was fired high into the air close to goal. A little gaggle of blue and red shirts jumped high in the air, their heads strained towards the spinning ball. Defenders and attackers clawed for dominance, each eager to make first contact with the ball.

There was no fog now, only one ginger head millimetres higher then the rest. One straining attacker so close to the ball. Her head pulled back, poised to strike, and . . . missed. Yes, missed the ball completely. The gaggle slumped downwards. All heads failed to make contact with their target. Bodies sagged ground-wards. Yet the ball fell too and brushed the shoulder of a downwards attacker. Almost in slow motion it spun towards the black mesh of the goal net. A lunging hand of the goalkeeper moved towards the ball. But the ball seeming to have a will and life of its own and flipped over the despairing outstretched gloved fingers to land firmly in the back of the net.

I was so proud of her. I was really really proud of Charlotte the footballer who had scored the goal to save the match in its dying seconds. Her strike was the one dazzle of sunlight which had cut through the foggy gloom of a December day. She told me to cut the crap.

'Stop going on about it, will you.'

'But it was your first goal for the club . . . and what a goal.'

'Yeah . . . I missed the header.'

'They all count.'

'A fluke.'

'Never . . . Sunday practice by the scrapyard pays dividend in the Saturday thriller.'

'Just shut up, will you.'

I couldn't. I wouldn't. For the whole week I had my head in the stars. We watched a video of the 1966 World Cup Final on Saturday night with the sound turned down so we could add our own commentary. Sunday was scrapyard practice, concentrating on free kick tactics. Monday was football magazine reading with insights into international stardom. And Tuesday . . . Well, Tuesday we had a row. Charlotte said she'd had enough of blooming football and if I as much as mentioned the word we were finished. So Tuesday and Wednesday I did a bit of private artistic preparation for the Saturday match in the way of banner painting.

The result of my efforts was a big sign with blue and black writing on a sheet smuggled out of the back bedroom saying

KICK IT UP
HEAD IT IN
CHARLOTTE

On Thursday I dribbled a can of baked beans round the legs of six customers, three shopping trolleys, down the frozen foods and dairy produce aisle, only to be given a yellow card and the warning of a full season suspension by Mrs Hillett. Some refs just want to spoil the game by their interfering stoppages. They should be encouraging young talent and a free-flowing end-to-end match. What the spectators want to see is the can being kicked right through the storeroom doorway to the cheers of the customers. But what do we get instead? Penalty after penalty and the wagging bony finger.

On Friday Charlotte found the banner and ripped it up, saying I'd 'really lost it' and if I ever brought anything along like that she'd walk off the pitch and never speak to me again. But I didn't mind. I was in good spirits and maybe the banner would have been difficult to fix to my bike for the ride to Park Grove.

On Saturday there was only one thing that mattered. One 90-minute, action-packed, ball-rolling, crowd-cheering, goal-scoring, titanic battle of skill, endeavour and daring. Yes! The Wanderers were once again gracing the turf of Park Grove.

Charlotte said it was only a friendly after several weeks of league matches, but I said, 'Friendly it may be, but it's still the chance to keep on the goal-scoring road. The pathway to success is only open to those with twinkling feet, hearts of oak and heads of steel.'

Charlotte said it should be a relaxed match and a bit of fun.

Marie was once again conspicuous by her absence. She'd sent the team a postcard with a picture of Old Trafford on it and a brief message saying: *Am talent spotting in the north. Back soon. Marie.*

The postmark was a bit smudged but it looked like Basingstoke which was only eight miles away. You certainly wouldn't find much talent in Basingstoke and it was south of us, not north.

I decided I'd do a mini-Marie. Not a 90-minute mobile verbal but a bit of encouragement on the touchline. The Wanderers needed support and the match crowd was small. In fact, it was microscopic. There were two sets of parents sitting in cars, a scruffy-looking dog with one ear, and me. Things certainly needed livening up.

I needn't have worried. For this was going to be one of the liveliest Saturday afternoons at Park Grove for some time.

It all began when the opposition, the Giants, ran out of the changing rooms and onto the pitch. You could see why the team got their name. Two of them were the biggest and tallest girls I have ever seen. One must have been nearly as tall as Blackpool Tower and the other, her twin, was even taller. She looked as tall as the Eiffel Tower. I felt dizzy just looking up at them both. The ground shook as they ran onto the pitch. The dog with one ear cocked his head on one side, barked and ran off.

The team gathered round in a kind of rugby scrum with Eiffel and Blackpool in the middle like tent poles.

I thought this was going to be exciting and that perhaps they'd got it all wrong and were going to play rugby. I'd never seen a match with one team playing football versus another team playing rugby before.

The Giants started to stamp their feet and shout a war cry like I once heard the New Zealand Rugby team do on TV. It was a disappointment when a few seconds later they started to kick the ball about and not pick it up and run with it.

The first incident happened after five minutes of play. The Wanderers had the ball when Eiffel stood on the foot of one of our players. It must have been like a three-ton truck running over you and the result was one limping player heading for the changing room. We were now reduced to ten and had no substitute to bring on.

Fifteen minutes later one of our star forwards, Sharon, was making a solo run towards the goal. She'd already beaten a couple of players and only Blackpool and the goalie stood between her and the goal. She made to go right, feinted and checked and clipped the ball past Blackpool on the left. All she had to do was to sprint left round Blackpool, regain control of the ball and crack it hard past the goalie. A doddle to go one-nil up.

Blackpool saw the plan just in time and lurched left. She made no attempt to play the ball and just obstructed Sharon's way. The two collided with Sharon sprinting fast. There was a nasty crunching noise and Sharon clattered to the deck, clutching her leg in agony.

Her mum came dashing out of her car, shouted abuse at Blackpool and carried Sharon off the pitch. Two minutes later her car sped out of the car park in a shower of dust and fury. It should have been the red card for Blackpool but the ref just bit her bottom lip and restarted the game. In the remainder of the half it was backing-off time. All of our players tried to keep a five-mile exclusion zone between them and the terrible tower twins.

At half-time they'd scored two goals and things looked grim. Our goalie had a sudden attack of nervousitis – I think it was called twin tower fever and – she left the pitch for the safety of the changing rooms. We now had eight players left and twin tower fever could strike again at any moment. In fact an epidemic was expected in the next three seconds.

I decided it was time for direct action and ran onto the pitch. I could be the sub, the hero to save the hour. I'd got my trainers and tracksuit on so there would be no stopping me.

Charlotte and I would team up to make searching raids into the Giants' goalmouth. We'd be fearless. The tower twins held no terror for our twinkling toes. We'd be too fast and clever for such lumbering mountains.

Charlotte wasn't too keen on the idea. She pushed me back in the direction of the touchline, shouting, 'No way. This is an all girls team and men are not allowed.'

Some of the players started to giggle. Charlotte still had hold of me and was pushing me further and further back towards the touchline.

Half as a joke one player said, 'Oh, let him play.'

There were more giggles.

'It's only a friendly,' said another. Groans and a few giggles.

'Go on, Chaz, it'll be a laugh,' said a third and turned to the ref, adding, 'What about a lad playing for us?'

The ref bit her lip and shrugged her shoulders. The question was asked again to the Giants.

'Who?'

'Him!'

'Him?'

'Yeah.'

More laughs from both lots of players. It was like picking teams on the beach, and I was the leftover nobody wanted. But I'd show them. They'd see.

Blackpool Tower stepped forward and looked me over like I was a second-hand pair of socks at a jumble sale.

'Only if *it* plays in goal,' she said with a growl.

There was a cheer from the Wanderers. I began to grin. Charlotte glared at me but I knew my chance had come.

The second half started straight away. We had quite a strong wind in our favour. I knew I had to take a big kick and smack the ball down into their goalmouth. If I could do this and try not to land it within a hundred miles of either tower we could be in with a chance. The trouble was that to start with nobody wanted to kick it back to me and there was a lot of fiddling-about sort of play in the middle of the pitch. Then one of the giants hoofed it upfield towards my goal. I came running out of my area and whacked it straight back downfield. But the wind was unpredictable and a sudden gust carried it high in the air and then far off to the left. It finally landed in a row of allotments.

By the time I'd gone to collect it and play had restarted we only had twenty minutes left before the final whistle. Still the play fiddled about in midfield with the remainders of the Wanderers running about in the opposite direction to the ball, trying to avoid the towers.

At last I received a long back pass. I waited for the ball to come to me and gathered it up close to my chest. I looked round the field and noted the positions of both towers. Charlotte was well downfield. I threw the ball up in the air, drew back my foot and hit it hard and true. Up it went like a rocket and then fell close to the goalmouth. Charlotte was there like an arrow. The ball bounced for a second time and then, with a crack of her head, she hit it fiercely into the back of the net.

Yes! Yes! Yes! No shoulder glance this time but a crisp sharp header right on target. I was ecstatic and ran about in the goal like a kid who's just got his first Christmas present.

We still had enough time. Enough minutes left to win the match. With the wind still blowing hard a repeat kick was all that was needed to draw level. After that a final onslaught would surely bring us victory. What a triumph it would be to snatch a win out of the jaws of failure.

I waited for the back pass or a hoof upfield but none came. Time was running out and our chances were diminishing by the minute.

'Kick it back . . . kick it back!' I screamed, but the wind drowned my cries. This was too much to bear. I knew what I had to do. It would be a risk but at this stage of the game there was no other choice.

I ran out of goal and down to the scrambling cluster of players in midfield. I tackled the first player and gained possession of the ball. I rounded a second and the goal was in sight. The towers advanced but I wasn't scared of them. My twinkling toes would be too fast for them. I feinted and dribbled, but on they came like a moving wall. All it needed was a little chip with the ball over them both and I'd be through.

I'm not sure exactly what happened next but somehow it all went wrong. I was sandwiched between the two. Squashed by Blackpool and Eiffel I fell to the ground like a burst paper bag. Blackpool had the ball at her feet. She steadied herself and drew back her foot. With enormous power she kicked the ball high over my head and into our goal – where I should have been.

I learned two things that afternoon at Park Grove – things I should have known all the time if I'd stopped to think about it.

The first was that it's no good being a selfish player, setting out to win the match single-handed. Football is a team game and if you forget that you could end up doing a nosedive on the turf like I did.

The second thing was to do with Charlotte – she was developing into a really good player. Soon she'll be playing in better teams than the Wanderers. Maybe she'll get a place in an England women's team. And what after that? The Premier Division? Once I would have thought that a ridiculous idea, but now I'm not so sure.

One Shirt Short of a Strip

Trevor Millum

Getting my kit right is a weekly problem. I always seem to have one bit missing. If I've got two boots and a pair of shorts and a shirt, guess what – no socks. Or one sock. Seems a silly thing to stop you playing – but you try wearing football boots without socks. Apart from anything else, you look a right wally.

My mum made her position clear a long time ago.

'Look,' she said. 'I don't mind washing your filthy kit. I don't even mind ironing it. But I will not look for it. If you don't put it out to be washed, I'm not going searching. I've got enough to do.'

Fair enough. But it meant that on a Saturday I'd be rummaging through my brother's cupboard looking for a shirt, or ringing Luke to ask if he'd got a clean pair of shorts I could borrow.

This Saturday was terrible. I rang Luke. I couldn't find my red top. I knew I'd brought it back last . . . well, whenever it was. It was essential. I'd been picked for the first team and I hadn't played with them for ages. It was against Bogdon's lot. They were going to play in white. Of course, I had a white shirt – but no red one.

Luke was no help.

'Don't tell me you've got problems,' he said. 'Me shorts are torn. I'll have to get me dad's and they're too big.'

Nor was Kev any better off.

'No,' he said. 'Can't find me boots. I may have left them at school or in Monty's dad's car. And he's in Wolverhampton. See you.'

I was frantic. I couldn't miss the match just for the sake of a red shirt. What could I do? Buy one? No money – and it wasn't worth the breath asking mum. I hadn't got the time to collect the pieces after she'd blown up.

Steal one? I admit I thought about it. But – never mind the morals – I didn't even know whose washing line to stalk.

Borrow one? I'd tried that. Everyone else that I knew was playing in red. Red shirts would be worth their weight in . . . well, red shirts, I suppose.

Make one? Now, don't be silly. Can you see me with a sewing machine and two metres of red cotton from the market?

Suddenly I had an idea. I did have a white shirt. And I did have enough money for some red dye, surely?

I met Luke in Mad Harry's where they sell everything.

'What are you after?' he asked.

'Red dye.'

He looked impressed.

'What about you?'

'Elastic,' he said and made a face. 'I got these old shorts but they're too big and they won't stay up. Need new elastic.'

That's how we came to be at my house after mum had gone out to Aunt Rachel's.

'Have a good game,' she said. 'I hope you win.'

She always said that.

Luke looked at the elastic, and then at the shorts. He looked lost.

'I think you'll need a needle,' I said helpfully. 'And some scissors.'

I had found my mum's sewing box. I wasn't quite sure how you put elastic in the top of shorts. It was a thing of mystery – unlike dying a white shirt red. That was obvious.

The instructions said that it could all be done in an hour. I ignored the bit about washing the garment first. I knew it had been washed at some point.

Water. Sink. Plug. Dye. This is easy, I thought.

It was quite good fun, too. I wondered why we didn't dye things more often. I thought of doing the net curtains.

I looked at the windows. The cat was sitting on the sill. A red and black cat would be something, eh? She gave me a look as if guessing what was in my mind. Maybe not. She's a fierce lady. So's Mum – so I dropped thoughts of cheering the place up with red curtains and concentrated on getting my shirt dry.

Luke was busy with scissors.

'What are you doing? You look like a surgeon or something.'

'I am a surgeon,' he said. 'I'm doing an elastectomy.'

I was impressed with that. He drew the old limp piece of elastic out of the shorts. He pulled back one end, intending to ping it at me. It snapped and the other end flicked him in the eye. 'Hmm,' was all he said.

He looked at the hole where the elastic had been and he looked at the long white band of new elastic. He started threading it through.

I was getting the rest of my kit together when the phone rang. It was Kev.

'No, I haven't got any spare boots,' I said. 'I've only just found my own.'

'Disaster!' he said. 'Disaster. Mega-disaster. Mega-mega-disaster . . .' I put the phone down. He couldn't be helped.

It took Luke half an hour to thread the elastic.

'I'm worn out,' he said. 'It's more tiring than playing football.' He looked at the two ends.

'You have to join them up,' I said.

He looked blank.

'I know that!' he said. But he still looked blank. I realized that he didn't know *how* to join the two ends.

'That's where the needle comes in. And thread. You sew the two ends together.'

Well, it sounds easy, doesn't it? We found some cotton. I even managed to thread it through the needle. But sewing wasn't something that I was good at. Neither was Luke.

'I should've listened when we did this in Technology,' he said. Eventually he did get the two ends to hold together. It was a botched job and the shorts didn't look much better than before.

'Still too loose,' I said. 'You'll have to try them on and see how tight it needs to be.'

For some reason Luke seemed unwilling to take his jeans off. We'd been in the changing rooms enough times so I couldn't see why. Maybe our kitchen felt different. Perhaps he thought the neighbours would be queuing up to see him in his underwear. Anyway, he took off his jeans in a very suspicious manner. Then I saw why.

'They're not mine,' he said.

Not only were his underpants several sizes too small, they were covered in bunny rabbits.

'Couldn't find mine,' he said. 'Had to borrow some of Wayne's.'

I think he was using the word borrow to mean 'take without asking'.

'They're very smart,' I said, trying not to laugh. He pulled on the shorts and yanked the elastic. It needed to be a lot tighter.

'I can't go through any more sewing,' he said. 'I'll tie it. It'll be better.'

'Don't do it too tight. What with those pants and that elastic, there'll be no blood getting to your legs.'

He put some kind of knot in the elastic, put his jeans back on and repacked the rest of his kit.

We left in a hurry. The shirt was just about dry and the shorts were just about safe. It started to rain on the way down but we didn't care. After the problems of the morning, we felt more than ready to face the opposition on the pitch.

'All right, boys?' asked Oggy. He was a sort of general purpose trainer and first aid man. He'd done a course once. He couldn't play football since his operation but he liked jogging about looking as if he mattered. 'Roger's reffing – so watch out. No bad language.'

We all knew Roger Ref. No sense of humour, that was his trouble. He sent Kev off once for wearing his spare shorts on his head.

'You got some boots, then, Kev?' I said.

He sighed. 'Me dad's,' he said. 'Miles too big.'

There was no time to worry about kit. This was it.

'All right, lads,' said Johnno, our captain. 'Let's play to win.' He had a strong way with words, did John.

'We're as good as them,' he went on, looking at me.

It was a tough match, no doubt about it. The rain really came down about ten minutes after kick-off.

35

My shirt stuck to me and I could feel trickles running down my skin. I didn't care; I was getting my share of the play, keeping myself in a good position, like I'd been told.

There was no score at half-time. We stood round in a dripping circle. One or two players looked at me a bit oddly. I thought it was because I didn't play in the team that often. Perhaps they were impressed by my playing. Perhaps they were a bit worried about the competition for places. I knew Kev and Luke, of course. And John – he lived down the street from me; went out training three times a week. That was a bit too serious for me. I had all my schoolwork to do, didn't I?

In the second half we really got cracking. John tore down the wing. I'd never seen him go so fast. It was a pity he didn't have the ball. Then Ginger crossed. There it was – two yards ahead of him, waiting to be tapped along by his nimble feet.

This was the chance. I was in a beautiful position fifteen yards from the goalmouth.

I saw him look around. The rain poured down. I didn't care. This was my chance – an opportunity that I wouldn't make a mess of. He stopped, swerved, looked around again and kicked. He crossed the ball – but not to me! What was he thinking of? The idiot. Was he blind? Had the rain got in his eyes? Or in his brain?

It bounced and landed near Kev. He was way off to the side but I knew he fancied his long curving kick. Just in off the post, he'd say. Well, here was his chance.

It was a mighty blow, all right. Wham! He thwacked it just in time. The ball shot towards the goal. Unfortunately, so did Kev's boot.

The ball hit the far post and didn't go in. The boot hit

the referee. No one could say it was Kev's fault. You couldn't do that kind of thing deliberately, though Roger Ref didn't see it quite like that.

It took a while for the game to get sorted out. When the ref is injured, who blows the whistle? Anyway, it wasn't a matter of life and death. A bit of a bruise above the eye. You've got to be prepared for that kind of thing when you're a ref.

Of course, he thought he'd been assaulted. He looked around to book someone. There wasn't anyone within five yards. Then he thought someone in the crowd had taken a shot at him. That wasn't very likely either. If anyone in the row of spectators on the touchline could throw that far they should be signed up straight away. Then he saw the boot.

He was still looking for a player with only one boot when Oggy Coach came on with his bag.

'What you doing, Oggy? Get off the pitch.'

'Injury, man.'

'I don't see anyone injured. I haven't blown the whistle.'

'It's you! You've been booted on the brainbox.'

'It's nothing.'

'Don't be daft. No fuss, now. Set a good example. Just an antiseptic wipe and a nice clean plaster. Have you up and about in no time.'

'I am up and about! Just leave me alone.'

In the end it was easier to let Oggy stick on the plaster and jog off the pitch looking pleased with himself.

Roger Ref was not pleased. Not only did he have a bruise on his brow, he felt that his dignity had been wounded. He looked again for a hopping footballer.

Kev hopped up. 'Sorry, ref,' he said. 'Wasn't my fault. Boot just came off. Too loose. Me brother's got me proper boots because he's playing in the match over at Baildon. I had to borrow these off me dad.'

'Shut up,' said Roger Ref. 'I don't want to know.'

He couldn't decide whether the rule book allowed him to book Kev or not. It was hard to think straight. 'Get your boot and put it back on,' he said. 'Just don't kick the ball like that again.'

He realized he hadn't blown the whistle to stop play. He blew. Everyone thought it meant play so the goalie booted the ball into midfield and there was a scramble of action.

'No no!' shouted Roger Ref. He blew again. 'Give me the ball!' he shouted.

'Why? What's up?' asked those who could hear him.

Someone rolled him the ball.

'What's wrong?'

'Nothing's wrong,' he said. 'It's just that I didn't blow to start – I blew to stop. The first time, I mean.'

'But we had stopped.'

'Yes, all right. But I hadn't officially blown the whistle to halt play.'

'But we knew to stop,' said Alex, who always knew everything. 'If the referee is struck by boot, clog, shoe or lightning, play must cease immediately.'

'But then you blew again,' said Tommo. 'Was that to start? Because we haven't. We've stopped.'

'Of course not! I mean, you'd started, so – anyway, that's not the point. We'll restart the match. Come on!'

He didn't tell anyone that he'd forgotten to make a note of how much time had been lost. About three minutes, he guessed. He hoped no busybody on the touchline had got a stopwatch for Christmas.

For some reason, Bogdon were given the kick-off.

Maybe because it was our side that had booted the ref.

The rain was easing off. There was half an hour to go. Every chance of a couple of goals. I bounced up and down a few times, trying to attract attention.

I noticed Luke was running in a funny way.

'What's up?' I called.

'Elastic,' he said. 'Gone again.'

'You look odd,' I said.

'You look right peculiar yourself,'

I didn't know what he was on about. He trotted off, one hand holding up his shorts. Served him right. He should've taken advice and not been so lazy. All the trouble I'd taken to make sure my kit was the right colour and he couldn't get a needle and thread together.

History was repeating itself. John had the ball again. I was in pole position. But he didn't seem to see me. What was I? Invisible?

Luckily Luke was coming up fast. John made a lovely cross. Luke leapt like a champagne cork.

Sadly, you can't leap like a champagne cork when you're holding your shorts up. So he let go. His leap was Olympic. It was also accurate. He connected with the ball and headed it like a professional. But as he went up, his rain-sodden shorts, heavy with water, went down. His shirt flapped in the wind. His shorts swayed round his shins and for a moment the rain seemed to stop, and the light seemed just right for everyone to get a perfect view of Luke's brother's bunny rabbit underpants.

I don't know if the roar from the crowd was for the goal, or the sight of the bunny rabbits. I didn't care. We all hugged him while he stood, squirming, trying to tie the elastic. It was hopeless – one end had disappeared.

Great goal, Luke! And great pants.

Luke isn't used to dealing with feelings. His face tried to cope with pride and embarrassment at the same time. In the end, he hoiked up the shorts, nodded a couple of times and trotted off.

We battled backwards and forwards in the rain and mud till the final whistle. I was tired and wet but I felt cheerful enough – though I was a bit miffed about the passes I hadn't had.

As we came off the field, I said, 'Told you to sew that elastic properly.'

'You can't talk,' he said. 'Look at you. All that trouble you went to and hardly a sign of it left.'

I looked down at my shirt for the first time. The colour had drained out. A few feeble streaks of red remained. Most of the remaining colour was on my legs. I looked as if I'd been boiled.

Of course John never sent a cross to me. From where he was, my shirt must've looked white. Never mind, Bogdon had passed to me half a dozen times. We'd won and I didn't care how wet or how red my legs were.

Mum did, though.

'I thought someone had been killed in our kitchen,' she cried. 'There's red everywhere. No, don't try cleaning it up yourself. Let me do it. Just don't *ever* ask me to wash that shirt!'

The Match

Robert Westall

They waited in Billy's yard for the football match to
start, for they hadn't a bean between them. They
might, like luckier boys, have parked their bicycles
against the sagging tarred fencing of Appleby Park,
and stood on their saddles and watched the match
over the top, free, at least till the man came. But they
had no bikes. They might, like others, have bored
holes with a brace-and-bit in the timber fence itself.
But they could no longer lay hands on a brace-and-
bit. Dads had become too wary. So all they could do
was sit patiently in Billy's yard, and listen to the
crowd's bellow coming through the warm muggy
autumn air, like the distant roaring of an enormous
lion.

All their hopes lay in the fact that the town's team
(called the Robins on a good day, and things unmen-
tionable on a bad) was inconsistent. It seemed to every
male inhabitant of the town, large and small, that
most teams in the North-Eastern League knew their
places in the League Table. Such grandees as Newcastle
Reserves and Sunderland Reserves reigned in glory at
the top, augmented thrillingly by ancient internationals
recovering from a leg injury or a bad night on the beer
and the manager's disfavour.

And the teams at the bottom, the Colliery Welfares,
knew their place too, with their madly sloping pitches

composed of cowpats and slag from the pit-heaps. But North Shields Robins could never make their mind up. They would shoot up the league table to third, inspiring the local paper to talk of appearing at Wembley. Then they would suddenly lose six games in a row, and plummet, and industrial production at the shipyards and guano-works would plummet with them, reducing the local reporters to wondering if Appleby Park shouldn't be sold up to build new houses on. And, when the team played badly, spectators walked out in disgust. Even before half-time. And left the gate swinging open for every small boy in the town to creep in. Whereas, if they were winning, the gate stayed tight shut right till the end.

'We should get in today,' said Sam. 'Blackhill are bottom of the league. And if we were to win, we'd go second too!' A broken staccato sound came winging over the chimneys. As of players being advised to knock the cowmuck off their boots, or get a set of crutches. Or go and decorate their wives' bedrooms.

'Blackhill's taken the field,' said Sam. They all nodded sagely. Then a happy roar. 'We've taken the field. And nobody's tripped over yet.' Then an acid storm of booing. 'The referee's come out.' And a groan. 'We lost the toss. Again.' They sat listening; and swaying in unison. A slow crescendo of joy. 'Charlie Blackstone. Dribbling down the right wing. Good old Charlie.' A scream of rage. Followed by a loud whistle. 'They tripped him up, the dirty swine. Penalty.' But the following buzz wasn't loud enough. 'Only a free kick.' A deep groan followed. 'And he's put it wide.' Finally, after many minutes, a jubilant roar.

'One-nil,' said Billy. 'To Robins. We'll never get in today now.'

'Wait,' said Sam. 'You know them . . .' And he was

42

right. Five minutes later, the sound of a huge animal dying in torment. 'Blackhill have equalized.' And soon, another dreadfully similar sound. 'Blackhill two, Robins one! Time to get moving, lads.' They hurried out, and up Hawkey's Lane. Halfway up, just after they had heard a third dreadful sound, they met a comfortably unbuttoned drunk. With a half-consumed froth-necked bottle in each pocket of his raincoat, and a football newspaper stuffed in each pocket of his sports coat. His tie was undone, and his trilby hat on the back of his head.

'Harry Mackintosh, of the *Shields Weekly News*,' said Sam, who was an expert. 'Off to write up the match. What's the headline this week, Harry?' The man bleared at them. ' "Robins crash to rampant Blackhill",' he said. 'But I know what it should be: "Bring in the death penalty for Vince Albrother." He missed two open goals. I don't know how he managed to miss the second. He was only a foot out. My granny coulda' done better.'

'Who does your granny play for, Harry?' asked Sam.

'Glasgow Rangers, you little tyke!' Harry aimed a blow at Sam's head, missed, and stayed upright by clinging to a lamp-post.

The next man they met was tearing his football programme into little tiny pieces, and strewing them like confetti. Albert started to pick them up, but everyone told him there'd be better programmes on the ground further on. There were. Some not even crumpled. There was another dire groan from behind the high, tarry wall, with its rusted advertisements for Bovril and Andrews Liver Salts.

'Vince's missed an open goal again,' said Sam philosophically. A long whistle went.

'Half-time,' said Sam. Ahead men were leaving the

gate in a steady stream, some pointing out lamp-posts convenient to hang Vince Albrother from. Quite a few men had a hand over their eyes, as at a graveside, and one was audibly weeping.

'You look forward to it all the week . . .'

'Mebbe there'll be tinned salmon for tea, George.'

'Aah couldn't eat a bite.' The gates were swinging open. They walked in. By this time they'd picked up about four perfectly unspoilt programmes each. Though what use they were . . . Still, they'd once cost threepence each.

'They don't give money back on them, do they?' asked Albert. They assured him not. 'But there's a raffle, Albert! The programme with the lucky number'll win!' It was a barefaced lie, but Albert began picking up every programme in sight.

It was a pleasant afternoon. The westering sun was shining on a green pitch, the cheery red jerseys of the Robins and the incredibly cheap scruffy-looking mustard jerseys of Blackhill Colliery Welfare. On the far side of the field the covered stand was in shadow, with a continuous flicker of flame as blokes lit up fags. The blokes in the stand, having paid more for their seats, were staying. But again Billy was lost in wonder that at every moment of the game, there was some bloke lighting up a fag. Maybe only when the Robins were losing . . .

There was a cripple on the touchline, offering Vince Albrother his crutches. There was a blind man, offering the referee his white stick and dark glasses. It must have had some effect. Vince Albrother fell down in the Blackhill goalmouth, and began writhing like a maggot in a bait tin.

'Foul,' yelled the remaining spectators, without hope. 'Penalty! Get your eyes checked, ref.' The referee blew his whistle very loud, to make up for blowing it very late. Vince Albrother took the penalty. Hit the crossbar with a terrible crack. The ball, by a miracle, rebounded to his feet. He kicked again, hit the crossbar another fearful smack. The rebound hit him in the chest this time, and trickled over the line for a goal.

'Goal,' shouted Sam, heroically, his small voice echoing around the ground in a lonely way.

'Not a proper goal,' said Nat. 'He frightened the goalie into surrendering. The goalie was lying on his face with his hands over his head.'

'Goal,' shouted Sam defiantly. He loved the Robins, and they gave him a lot of pain.

The Robins' third goal was even more ridiculous. The Blackhill forwards were hammering away at the Robins' end so hard that Sam had hidden his eyes down behind the billboards in his anguish. And the Blackhill goalie had drifted up the field to watch the fun. Except that the fun had been going on quite a long time, and the goalie had drifted a very long way from his goal. So when the Robins' goalie got his hands on the ball, and gave it the hugest possible kick to give himself some peace . . . The ball bounced. Clean over the Blackhill goalie's head. It then went on bouncing majestically down the field with the Blackhill goalie in hot pursuit. Ten yards out, he nearly caught up with it. Then he tripped, and fell on his face. The ball paused on the goal-line. As if suddenly nervous. And then a gust of wind blew it over. After that, Vince Albrother became like a man inspired. The final result was 4–3 to the Robins. And as the boys turned to go, they saw that, miraculously, the ground was full again. Not only had the original spectators returned, drawn by more hopeful sounds travelling across the warm air and the black chimney-pots, but there were also men who'd been out walking their dogs and families with little kids, and even housewives in carpet slippers and their hair in curlers.

'Well done, Vince,' shouted one of them. 'You know where to put it, don't you?'

The Brylcreemed Vince gave her a lascivious grin and said, 'I'll be down for me supper, Ma.'

'And I'll give you a good hot one,' said the lady, not to be outfaced.

Meanwhile, Albert had picked up every programme in sight. He was carrying a pile of programmes so high, he could hardly see over the top of them. He had bundles stuffed in every pocket.

'One of them's *bound* to have the lucky number,' he said. 'I'm off to collect my winnings.' They watched him vanish up the wooden stairs of the club building.

'Poor swine,' said Henry. 'They gave up having a lucky number on the programme a year ago.'

'It kept him quiet. It kept him happy. So he didn't ask daft questions all the time.'

'He needs something to keep him occupied.'

'By gum, I'd like to be a fly on the wall in there. Bet he comes out flaming berserk.' But in the end Albert came out smiling, without the programmes. He held out a filthy hand, and showed them a worn threepenny bit.

'That's not a *prize*!' gasped Sam.

'No. He gave it to me for picking up all the litter. Says I've saved him half-an-hour. And his back's playing up something cruel today.'

The gang eyed the threepenny bit avidly.

'Chip shop'll be open, Albert!'

'Bag o'chips all round, and *two* for you!'

Albert clenched his fist round the coin, as if he was going to argue.

'Picking up the programmes was our idea, Albert!' said Billy, asserting his authority. Albert eyed them, then nodded. It was four to one. Even he could count that much. On the way down town to the chip shop, Sam said: 'Hey, I hope somebody phoned up Harry Mackintosh, and told him the final result!' But when they got out of the queue at the chip shop, the paper-lads were already shouting around their Sporting Pinks: 'Robins crash to rampant Blackhill.'

'They'll sack him for sure now,' said Henry, worried. 'Garn. He does it all the time.' They had a good laugh. All but Billy. He walked along deep in thought. Vince Albrother, making all those mistakes, being hated by everybody. But keeping on trying. And winning in the end. Albert, picking up all those pro-grammes for nowt, and then getting threepence out of nowhere. Albert, stupid though he was, had won too. He thought about certain school lessons. Aesop's fable about the tortoise and the hare. Robert the Bruce and the spider. He had always thought till now that all victories were well planned, glorious, a foregone con-clusion. But that wasn't the way that victory had come to Albert, or Vince Albrother. Maybe you won just by going on. Staying hopeful.

Misfits

Gina Douthwaite

Ben Boswell's hands were black. The print from the papers had really mucked up his Ferrets shirt.

'Shan't be watching *them* again,' he sighed, rubbing at the smudges as he slotted a copy of *Southdown Times* through the last letterbox. 'Oh, why did we have to move?'

Ben had asked so many 'whys' since his mum and dad had split. He thrust his hands deep into the canvas bag. Fingers closed on a leftover copy.

'Oh no, I've missed one!' His mind buzzed back over the route, trying to recall each delivery; but he was new to the place, couldn't picture each gate, each house, each tree-lined road. He shivered a little as an early finger of autumn rippled the leaves. 'I'll just have to backtrack,' he groaned.

The gravelly drive? Yes, he'd certainly crunched up there.

He'd BEWARE-d OF THE DOG next door and almost been wagged to death for his efforts.

The flats in the dark house? That was it! They shared a letterbox, but he'd pushed only one paper through. He remembered now. He'd rushed away. Hadn't liked that feeling of being watched from behind grimy windows.

'Oh well, here goes.' And with eyes fixed on the newsprint he crept up to the step. '*Under 14s' soccer* tournament,' he read as he started to feed it through. 'Anyone interested report to Southdown Park, Saturday at—' With that the door snapped open and a hand shot out, snatching the paper.

''Bout time too!' scratched a weasely voice. But the door slammed before Ben had time to explain.

'Wish I was back with my dad, back with my mates,' he sniffed, kicking a stone down the hill. He booted it into the alleyway between the houses, passed it to the fence on the wing, picked up the return and scored between the trees on the Green.

'Goal!' he yelled, but instead of the roar of a crowd and a mass invasion of the pitch just one angry voice roared from its patch of garden.

'Watch what you're doing, lad. We don't want louts like you around here.'

'I don't want to be here! I don't want to be here!' Ben felt the words choking in his throat.

With shoulders slumped he pushed home through the bushes to 13, Snicket Close.

After Saturday morning papers he dashed to Southdown Park, and stood looking through the railings. It wasn't only the bars that separated him from the lads in stripes and hoops who were passing and posing, and boasting of brand new boots. He rubbed at the smudges on his shirt, making them worse. There hadn't been time to wash. The sole was flapping from his trainers. His tracksuit bottoms were torn. Ben's spirits drained away, deep into his shadow.

A whistle blew. Someone blasted out orders. The kids in the park swarmed towards the sound.

'You going in?'

Ben turned. He saw a face of freckles capped by a

crop of red hair. The grin challenged him. 'Come on,' she said. 'I want to play, don't you?'

'Sure,' he rumbled, his voice suddenly deeper. Ben cleared his throat. Had that really been *him*?

He started to amble across as though it didn't matter. 'Come on!' she urged, skipping sideways. 'You'll miss your chance.' And flipping a skinny hand at him she charged off into the crowd.

Ben was left on the edge. The others were shoving and sorting, dividing into groups. Someone's fingers clamped on his wrist. Someone else's pulled them away.

'We've got enough now,' a voice said.

Ben backed off. He saw a crop of red hair tear towards a distant pitch. *She* was part of a team.

He retreated to the railings. The odd one out, again.

In the dim front bedroom of Number 13, Ben was scribbling away. By midnight he'd got it right and had written it out forty-three times on gaudy paper, which he'd saved for something special:

TRAIN WITH THE
MISFITS
CHALLENGE TEAM

If you're soccer mad
and under 14
meet Sunday night
on
Snicket Green
(6 p.m. for kick-off 6.15 p.m.)

He fell asleep chanting the words in his head like a rap.

*

Next morning the world was Sunday-quiet apart from a paper boy who dribbled an unseen ball up and down the sun-shot streets. His spirits were up in the trees today, dancing with the leaves.

Wherever he saw a ball in a garden, a bike slung against a wall, a soccer shirt on a line or any sign of 'under 14' life, Ben slipped a Misfit notice in with the Sunday paper.

'Right on target!' he grinned as the forty-third gaudy sheet was handed to a spotty lad who was flumping a flattened ball against a wall.

'What's this?' asked Spotty, with disinterest.

'Did you try for the teams in the park yesterday?'

'What? Me? You must be joking. They wouldn't want *me*.' And Spotty wumphed the airless plastic into the road.

'I do. Look.' Ben pointed to the leaflet. 'Let's get our own team. Let's show 'em, eh?'

Spotty looked. Chewed his lips. Looked back at Ben. 'OK. I'll be there. Have you got a ball?'

'I will have,' stated Ben with such belief that he knew it would happen.

Somehow, it would.

Ben pushed his empty newspaper sack over the counter.

Mr Mace looked at the youngster. He should really check on his age. But, no, the boy worked too well to risk losing him.

'Thanks, Ben. Any problems?'

'Not with the papers, thanks, Mr Mace.'

The newsagent peered over his glasses, 'But . . .?' he prompted.

'I . . . I need a football.'

'A football?'

'Yes, by six o'clock.'

'Six o'clock, eh?' said Mr Mace thoughtfully. 'Might I ask why?'

Ben told his story.

Mr Mace listened, then rummaged under the counter. 'See this key?'

Ben nodded.

'Go and unlock the shed. You might find what you want in there.'

Ben lowered his head and looked at the floor. 'Thanks,' he mumbled, 'but . . .'

'A lot of "buts" around this morning,' teased Mr Mace. 'It's not stock for the shop, Ben, so don't worry about . . . Well, just don't worry. Go and have a look, eh?'

Ben reached for the key and edged through to the back.

A neat click and turn and Ben stepped into the shed where a warm, woody smell swept round him. His fingers shuffled through rusty nails, ran over oily rags. As he turned towards a wall of trowels and forks his shin collided with a bike pedal. Bending down to rub his leg better he saw it under the bench – a dusty football, grey with age. He coaxed it out. Tossed it. Turned it. Hugged it to his grubby shirt.

'All we need now is a team.'

At two minutes to six Ben pushed through the bushes at number 13. He'd been watching from the bedroom window. Snicket Green at 6 p.m. on a Sunday was usually deserted, but not this Sunday. Excitement stabbed in his stomach as he strolled up the Close, the ball tucked under his arm. There was Mick Smith from up the road, leaning against a tree, his socks wrinkling into too-big boots. Mick was swaying with the sapling trunk and thumping a fat friend.

'Hiya, Ben!' he yelled. 'Do y'know who's doing this Misfit thing?'

'No,' said Ben. Who didn't know why he'd said 'No', but suddenly felt much safer. 'I've just brought a ball, that's all.' He shrugged his shoulders and looked around as though for a leader.

A lad with bandy legs yelled, 'Pass it, then!'

'Yeah, come on. Let's get started. I'm not missing my tea for nothing.' Mick's fat friend wobbled with enthusiasm, and a squib of a kid punched the ball out of Ben's arms. The spotty boy wumphed it away.

Kick-off – 6.15

Short-sighted lads with glasses shot at the wrong goals, nutters headed it heavenwards, a boy with one short leg ran in circles making everyone dizzy, sneaky foulers rolled and groaned like star actors and a face of freckles skipped sideways up the wing.

'You got chosen!' accused Ben, when they tussled for a throw-in.

'Wouldn't want to play for those softies,' grinned the red-headed Edwina. 'I'm joining Misfits.'

And the Misfits did seem to fit. Even the duff ones blocked the shots, and some of the belters were brill!

So Sunday night on Snicket Green saw the sowing of seeds for a Misfit team.

It also brought the residents out into their gardens. Songs of praise were not on their lips this Sunday tea-time.

'Just watch my roses!' wailed Mr Pickles.

Poor Specky with the squint had spied a lamp-post,

seen it as a goalpost, and 'scored' in Mr Pickles' rosebed.

'Sorry,' squinted Specky, tripping over the kerb in his haste to retrieve the ball. 'Sorry – sir.'

Mr Pickles was impressed. 'Sir.' It suited him well. This boy had manners, and the roses were undamaged. 'Sir' handed back the ball. 'Postbox behind the goal. Red,' he snapped. 'Aim for that.'

'Thank you, sir,' squinted Specky and on the turn booted the ball at the box.

'*Yes!*' Mr Pickles' arms shot in the air, and all the neighbours watched, agog.

Skinny Flint took it on the rebound. He whizzed up the wing, then centred. 'Yours, Boss!' he yelled.

Ben Boswell chested it down with pride, curved it round Buster and flicked it to Nuttall. Nuttall's neck extended like that of an ostrich. One nod and the ball bounced between Bandy's legs.

'*Goal!*'

All the Misfits ran to Nuttall and hoisted him shoulder high.

'H-up, H-up, H-up,' they cheered, while Boot sent the ball into the sky. It landed with a dreadful shattering sound.

The cheering stopped and the Misfits fled – up the path, into bushes, under cars – before thin Miss McKinney appeared, clutching her Siamese cat.

Many pairs of Misfit ears, hidden, heard a *Yowl!*

Many pairs of Misfit eyes saw a *Leap!* . . . just as Mr Carter's car was coming up the road.

Mr Carter didn't see the cat, didn't see Springer hurtle from behind the hedge and save the Siamese from an instant skinning.

But Miss McKinney did.

'Gracious, gracious,' fussed Miss McKinney,

forgetting about the shattering sound that had brought her to the door. She buried her face in the champagne fur of the purring cat and muttered her way back home.

The Misfits emerged one by one.

'Saved our skins there, Springer.'

'Brilliant bit of catkeeping, Springer.'

'Springer for goalie, Springer for goalie!'

The chant was gathered up, but as others chipped in something began to happen:

'Springer for goalie.'

'Nuttall's up front.'

'Fowler's all over doing his stunts.'

'Flint can be winger.'

'Spotty for spot.'

'Buster's a back and Specky's best shot.'

'Bandy's a boost curving corners in sharp.'

'Dizzy's in midfield.'

'Ed'll add spark.'

'Boot must be sub because Boot has lost Ben Boswell's ball and Ben is the *boss*.'

So the Misfits had picked their first team from a mightily messy display of undisciplined booting about. With less than a week before the local tournament, training had to start in earnest, and Ernest was to be their coach – Ernest Pickles who, in his lost youth, had played for Southdown Wonders.

Ernest Pickles rose to the task of training the Misfits with dignity, and with the donation of a ball.

On Monday at six all the Misfits met on Snicket Green and all the curtains twitched in Snicket Close.

'Let's get warmed up first,' ordered Pickles. 'What about a gentle jog around the Green.'

Fat lads and leggy lads and tied-in-knots-no-hopers

set off in a rush like a gush of water, which halfway round had thinned to a trickle. The lean and lanky soon lapped the fat and gasping, whom Pickles had to pull in before they collapsed completely.

'Something less taxing, I think,' thought Pickles, surveying the heap of heaving bodies.

'Boswell!' he boomed. 'Bring 'em in.' And Ben, who was still jogging with the fitter Misfits, led them to the centre.

'Get your breath, boys. Get ready for a little light limbering. Ready... and skip... and hop... and bend those knees...'

'Mr Pickles, may I have a word?'

Ernest Pickles bristled. He recognized the smooth tones of his neighbour, Ms Fairfax.

He turned. 'Yes, dear lady. How can we help you?'

'It's more a case of how I can help you, Mr Pickles,' soothed Ms Fairfax in her leotard. 'I've been watching.'

'Are you interested in, er, soccer?' he asked, warily.

'I'm interested in keeping these young people alive. They seem a little stressed.'

Pickles looked at the flushed and sweating bodies. 'Not fit. Not yet,' he retorted.

'Allow me,' she crooned, and spread her arms wide:

'Lie back, lads, and listen to me.
Inside your heads, picture the sea...'

This was met by waves of sniggers and snorts but Ms Fairfax rippled on, lulling them into a trance:

'... now float away upon the sea
inside your head – feel light and free.'

And soon, only snuffles and snores ruffled the ocean of laid-back bodies.

'They're not here to go to sleep!' hissed Pickles.

Ms Fairfax put her finger to her lips. 'Just a few minutes,' she whispered. 'Then dismiss them. I'll see the Misfits tomorrow.'

And she did, but not until Pickles had limbered up limbs and elasticated sluggish sinews, and not until the 'dangerous dog' from up the road had joined them in their jogging. All the Misfits ran much faster round the Green this time.

So sweat poured and muscles were toned on Tuesday, and even Ernest Pickles and the dangerous dog lay down with the rest when Ms Fairfax drifted over to do her bit for the Misfits.

'How's it going, Ben?' asked Mr Mace, counting out Wednesday's evening papers.

'It's great! Sorry about your ball, though.' He glanced up, feeling guilty about the loss of the ball which had smashed Miss McKinney's window. She'd displayed the deflated trophy from the front bedroom: a warning as to the fate of errant missiles.

'Can't help out with another, I'm afraid,' he said. 'But what about this?' Mr Mace picked up a leaflet from the counter and passed it to Ben.

CAR BOOT SALE
Friday, 13th
6.30 p.m.
Southdown Wonders Ground

'That's the day before the tournament,' said Ben. 'But what's it got to do with me?'

'Raise some cash for the Misfits,' suggested the newsagent. 'Get them all to bring something from home. We'll take my car, set up a stall and . . .'

'Well thanks, Mr Mace,' mused Ben, studying his fingers, 'but after Saturday it'll all be over.'

'Surely not!' protested Mr Mace. 'You'll keep on playing, won't you? And anyway,' he added cautiously, 'what about the entry fee?'

'Entry fee?' Ben hadn't thought about an entry fee! Nor had he thought about the Misfits' future.

'Friday.' He looked at the leaflet again. 'We haven't got a practice, Friday. *Right*! We'll do it!'

All day Thursday, Misfits of various shapes and sizes descended upon the newsagent's shop to present offerings for the car boot sale.

Springer handed over his Mr Sleepy alarm clock.

'Don't need it now,' he announced. 'Can't wait to get up in the morning.'

Spotty squeezed past the regular customers to donate a bar of anti-spot soap. 'They're going,' he grinned. 'No time for picking now. I'm kicking that into touch!'

Flint came in giving a last flick to his cigarette lighter. 'Never did enjoy them,' he muttered, and went out again.

A big bag of broken biscuits was delivered with great ceremony by Buster who made quite a point of adjusting his jeans and tightening his belt.

'D'you think this'll sell?' asked the ostrich-necked Nuttall as he took off his baseball cap.

Mr Mace stroked the feather that was stuck in the band. 'That's a real feather in your cap, lad,' he said, sensing Nuttall's reluctance to part with it. 'Perhaps you can buy it back, later.'

'What time does the sale start?' asked Nuttall, his eyes wide with hope.

'Half past six, half past six,' rapped Dizzy, coming in clicking his fingers and holding a pair of odd shoes. A pair because there were two. Odd because one had a built-up heel to lengthen Dizzy's shorter leg.

'Sick of these.' He plonked them onto the counter. 'See you at six, last practice . . .' And off he went, clicking his fingers and chanting.

Before the shop closed, Fowler had given his whistle. 'No need to blow my own any more,' he quipped. 'Ref blows every time I go near the blooming ball. Need my puff for running, anyway.'

'Thanks, Fowler!' said Mr Mace. 'Can you hold the door for Bandy?'

Bandy was struggling in with a huge pair of bongos. 'Can't wedge these between my legs any more. I'm sure they've straightened out!'

'Could use them to drum out the news,' grinned Mr Mace.

'The news is we're late,' interrupted Fowler. 'Come on, Bandy.'

And the two shot off to meet Boot on the way to Snicket Green.

Boot was dribbling a heavy, leather ball.

'Where'd you get that?' asked Bandy, as Fowler tripped Boot from behind and raced off with the prize.

Boot sped after him, tackled cleanly and left his pal rolling in 'agony' in the gutter.

Bandy was so busy giggling he failed to see the back pass. It lodged between his calves. His legs hadn't let him down after all.

'Where'd you get it?' he repeated.

'It's for the boot sale,' cracked Boot. 'Boss can take it tomorrow.'

Ben was on the Green, watching Edwina practising headers.

'Try this!' yelled Boot, launching the ball.

Edwina rose to the challenge, but crumpled under the impact. The ball dropped. Only Nuttall's neck contortions kept it in the air. He nudged it on to Specky.

Ernest Pickles seized the ball. 'Split into two, you lot,' he ordered. 'Let's get on with it.'

With one ball for Ben's team and one for the dangerous dog's, they headed and tackled and dribbled and passed and shot as badly as a bunch of blind bears.

There was dire despair on the Green that evening.

'We're cursed,' moaned Ben Boswell. 'We're cursed.'

His eye shifted to three shadowy figures at the upstairs window of 7, Snicket Close.

'Look!'

'Where? Which house?' hissed Specky.

'Exactly. Witch House,' wailed Flint, and the hackles on the dangerous dog bristled as the curtains closed.

No matter how Ms Fairfax tried to soothe them into sailing away that evening, all they could do was picture witches inside their heads and hear their voices, cursing.

'Here's a ball from Boot,' said Ben, early Friday morning. He rolled it over the counter. 'Oh, and a shirt from me.'

'*Stokes.*' Mr Mace read the name printed across the back of the shirt.

'Yeah! Sean Stokes. He captained Ferrets the year they won the cup.'

Ben's voice was choked with pride.

'Sure you want to give this, Ben? It must mean a lot.'

'I'm sure.'

'Then why the pained face?'

Ben explained how useless they'd been last night.

'Last practice,' he huffed, 'and we just couldn't connect.'

'That's the way it goes,' soothed Mr Mace. 'It'll all come together tomorrow.'

'Not if we're cursed,' he muttered under his breath, but it felt a bit silly to tell of witches, here, on a sunny day.

When the shop shut, Ben and Mr Mace drove to Southdown Wonders' Ground. They set out their wares with care: the Ferrets shirt swung in the wind from the tailgate.

'Something's missing,' puzzled Mr Mace, looking at the goods and scratching his head. 'What . . .?'

He leaped into the air, hitting the tailgate with his head as Springer's alarm clock sprang into action from the back seat of the car.

'We'll have to sign it up,' laughed Ernest Pickles, who'd just arrived with several stems of roses to sell. 'Hope the sale goes well. I'm off to meet some old team-mates now. Don't be late tomorrow, Ben.'

Ben backed out of the car with a box of old *Beanos*. 'Think I'll take Mr Sleepy with me, just to make sure,' he joked, still trying to find how to silence the clock.

By 6.35 p.m. Nuttall had reclaimed his cap and given 50p for the privilege, the biscuits had been bought and much rummaging was taking place. *Beanos* were browsed, bongos banged, and soap was sniffed. All was bustle and fun till somebody lifted the ball.

'That's ours!' stormed an angry voice. 'Where'd you get it?'

'It's ours,' objected Ben, not mentioning Boot's name but, nevertheless, beginning to wonder ...

'Look here.' The youth stabbed a finger at the stitching. 'S'bin mended, see. Splits at the seams, dun it. Left it at Boot's Cobblers, Wednesday, di'n I.'

Boot's Cobblers. Is that Boot's dad's? Ben's thoughts were connecting. *He must have 'borrowed' it from the shop! Blimey, Boot. That was a daft one.*

'It just got given,' muttered Ben, turning red.

'Yeah, well it just got given back,' snarled the youth, bouncing it fiercely on the ground. 'Yeah?'

'Yeah,' agreed Ben, meekly.

Ben's meekness soon turned to rage, however, as the ball was tossed to a gang of lads, who all looked back, and jeered.

'Ferrets shirt's sold,' said Mr Mace, placing a hand on Ben's shoulder. He felt sad for the lad.

'Who to?' asked Ben, half-heartedly. There was no one near.

'Big chap. Said he was sure it would fit. Gave us a twenty-pound note!'

'Brilliant!' grinned Ben, brightening up. 'Then we've done it? We've raised enough for the entry fee?'

'We've done it, Ben, ball or no ball. And so will the Misfits.'

Ben knew he should have said, 'Thanks', but he couldn't. It had something to do with a lump, the size of a football, that was sticking in his throat.

Ben woke at 6.30 a.m. on Tournament Day. He'd set Springer's alarm clock for 5.30 but was soon to learn that no matter what time it was set for, it always rang at 6.30.

With the paper round behind him and the Tournament in front, Ben pushed through the bushes at number 13. Excitement stabbed in his stomach as he strolled to Snicket Green.

There was Mick Smith leaning against a tree. There was Ms Fairfax in her leotard, thin Miss McKinney with the Siamese cat, the dangerous dog with its owner on a lead, three black-clad figures from number 7, and every Misfit who'd ever trained on Snicket Green.

Every Misfit, that is, but Ernest Pickles.

'Where's Pickles?' someone asked.

'Yeah, where *is* he?'

Heads turned.

Ears burned as nervous whispers started:

'He's let us down.'

'Thursday did it!'

'This is a pickle!'

'Let's go without him.'

'Hang on a minute . . . *Hang on a minute!* Isn't that Pickles?'

And it was Pickles, staggering behind a bulging black bin-liner.

'Team kit!' he announced with pride as an avalanche of shirts tumbled from the bag.

'Red and white!' whistled Fowler. 'Southdown Wonders wore red and white yonks ago.'

'Not that many yonks,' stressed Pickles, demonstrating a pass on a non-existent ball.

Something was beginning to fit.

'But where did you get them?' asked Bandy.

'Car boot sale. My mates were manning the Wonders' stall. Got a real bargain.'

'A real bargain. *Yes!*' And all the arms on Snicket Green shot into the air.

Mr Mace waved from behind the counter as the Misfits passed by on their way to Southdown Park.

'I'll be shutting shop at twelve today,' he told his customer, handing over the *Saturday Sport* and change from a £20 note.

'Interesting lot of lads,' remarked the man.

Mr Mace explained.

The big chap turned to leave, revealing the name *Stokes* in print across his back. 'Maybe I'll see you there,' he said.

And maybe he did, but the big chap with the *Saturday Sport* was keeping a keen eye on the kids in the long and floppy, red and white shirts.

'You're doing *wonders*,' praised Ernest Pickles.

They'd beaten the Clucking Cockerels (whose performance had earned them the nickname 'Dozy Roosters' – among other things), and Fowler had wrenched a vital penalty shot from the gullible Goats, tossing aside their hopes of a winning goal.

Now they faced the final. The Snatchers – captained by the big lad from the boot sale – were already out there, booting about with a heavy, leather ball.

'What a load of cobblers,' they jeered as the Misfits hobbled onto the field, flagging with fatigue.

The team tried its best.

The three black-clad figures cast their spells and chanted from the line, but it did no good. They weren't real witches and couldn't even curse properly.

Even a magic charm could not have put back the zing in Springer's limbs. When the shots came there was little the Misfits' goalie could do but stretch, and wave them through.

Snatchers 2 – Misfits 0

At half-time Ms Fairfax ignored the jeers as she tried

to coax the Misfits to 'Lie back and listen', but all that was floating away was the final and their chance of triumph. And so the tension grew . . .

Ben led his team through a second half of relentless attack. Try as they might, the only thing to hit the back of the Snatchers' net was Miss McKinney's escaping Siamese. As the goalie made to pick it up and kick it into play, *yowls* abounded. The cat had scored, if only with its claws.

Pickles and the dangerous dog joined forces to bark instructions. The Snatchers' snider tactics were to mock the Misfits. With only minutes to go, their endless taunting of Specky's squint drove the lad to see red. He scored from sheer rage! In the ensuing excitement the dog broke free, took possession of the ball and equalized as the final whistle blew.

Snatchers 2 – Misfits 1 (dog 1)

The Misfits had lost. They cheered wearily as the Snatchers' loud-mouthed captain received the trophy, and £20, from a large man in a Ferrets shirt.

Ben rushed to the shop for his papers. He scrambled them into his bag. Something brushed his shoulder.

'If you deliver your papers, lad, as well as you do a ball,' tapped the big chap with the *Saturday Sport*, 'then Mr Mace is going to miss you.'

'Miss me? What do you mean?' asked Ben, thinking he'd lost his job. 'I am old enough . . . soon.'

'You're old enough now,' laughed the talent scout. 'Maybe not for papers, but you're old enough to train. And one day you might sign for Ferrets, young man – like I did. You see, Sean Stokes was once a Misfit like you.'

The Bottom Line

David Harmer

'Rats,' said Tom bitterly. 'Rotten two-faced, sneaky, slimy, stinking, rats.'

There was a moment's silence. Then Dekko said, 'Have we done something to offend you, Tom?'

Tom was so angry he could hardly reply. Something to offend me . . . something to. . . .'

'You seem a bit upset,' said Lee.

'Upset? You bet I'm upset.'

Lee looked puzzled. 'Why?'

'I'll tell you why, Lee. Because two days ago I had a football team for the five-a-side and now I haven't. You've all left me. You're all in Dixon's Dynamos now. Rotten rats.'

Lee looked hurt. 'But you were ill, we didn't know you were coming back today.'

'I only had a cold.'

'You never. You had Viral Globular Raging Red Spots. That's serious, that is.'

'I had *what*?'

'Don't know,' said Dekko, 'but Robert Dixon said you had it.'

'And that you'd be off school for *weeks*,' added Gurteak.

'So we all thought we'd take up his offer and join his team,' said Lee.

'There's no such thing as Globular Thingy Red Spots

or whatever you said. He made it up to pinch you lot off me!'

'Too late now,' said Dekko. 'We've promised.'

It was the summer term at Riverside Junior School and that meant the school five-a-side competition organized by Mrs Salt, the head teacher, and Mr Jardine, the deputy. Years 5 and 6 made up one competition and Years 3 and 4 another. The rules were simple; just the normal football rules, apart from no offside, and the goalie being helped out in defence by a semi-circular area into which no other player could go. Of course, the pitch was less than half a full-size one.

The only other difference was that because Mr Jardine had persuaded Mrs Salt to buy some fancy goals, they used proper five-a-side nets with a low crossbar. The teams had both boys and girls in, and in the case of a draw after five minutes each way, there would be penalties. Mr Jardine did the refereeing and Mrs Salt was on crowd control, something which came very easily to her. There were two cups, one per competition, and medals to be won. It was a very popular event.

Tom was in Y6J. He had organized one of the strongest teams, Bell's Sharpshooters, until Robert Dixon's dirty work had mugged him.

He saw Robert that morning during break.

'I honestly thought you were ill, Tom.' Robert's eyes were as round and as wide and as big as the lies that tumbled out of his smiling face. 'But I'm glad you're better now. Pity about your team, but it's good that the others have got a game. They might've missed out altogether.'

Tom was not a violent boy, but the temptation to shove Robert Dixon's crisps right down his cocky little throat was strong, only stopped by the fact that Robert's throat, like the rest of him, wasn't that little really and that Mr Jardine was on yard duty at the time.

'Don't worry, Tom,' said the teacher. 'Nothing starts until next week. I'm sure you could put a bit of a team together. Bound to be someone wanting to play who's not found a side.'

The one good thing left to Tom was that Kerry, with her dazzling right foot, had remained loyal. 'They've got Tracy Hardwick playing,' she said. 'She's my mate. I wasn't going to push her out. Robert tried to con me into his team but I knew I'd get a game somewhere.'

Then, after a day of guilt, Gurteak sheepishly came back. But there was no shifting Dekko and Lee.

We're on the books now, Tommy,' they said. 'Us two, plus Tracy and Joe Spenser.'

'Books?'

'Yeh, Robert's mum's let us have free sweets from their shop for a week if we play for him.'

'So we're on wages now,' said Lee, 'unless you've got a better deal.'

'Like free chocolate,' said Dekko. 'She won't let us have that.'

'Get lost, you two,' said Tom. 'Just get lost.'

'We will. You've got Viral Thingy,' they chanted. 'It's like the Dreaded Lurgy only ten times worse.' Giggling, they ran off.

'Take no notice,' said Kerry. 'We'll find someone.'

On Thursday things brightened up a bit when Craig Ward from Year 5 came back from a holiday in Majorca and needed a team to join. He was a very useful goalkeeper. In fact, he had played for the school team when Dekko had pulled a wheelie on his bike as he went round the corner of McMillan Avenue at the same moment as Ron Rose the milkman walked round it from the other direction. The result had been very messy indeed, with milk, glass and Dekko's bike all over the road. Dekko had been off school for two weeks and Craig had played well in his place.

But Friday came, the competition was due to start on the following Monday with Bell's Sharpshooters drawn against Dixon's Dynamos, and there was still no fifth player on the horizon.

Tom was on the point of giving up, but Mrs Salt had other ideas.

After assembly that morning Tom found himself in her office, being seated on the comfortable chair in the corner and smiled at in a way he recognized. Mrs Salt had two smiles. One went with the comfortable chair and meant that he was doing OK and that he was on the right side of the fence. The other smile was a lot nastier, contained no comfortable chair, and meant a lot of trouble. Fortunately, this seemed to be the first.

'Tommy, Mr Jardine tells me that you're having problems finding a fifth player for the competition?'

'Yes, Mrs Salt,' he replied dutifully, wondering where all this was going. Mrs Salt wasn't one to mess around.

'Well, you'll be pleased to know that I've found you a player.'

Tom's sudden rush of hope that Lee was about to give up the free sweets and return, were dashed on the rocks of Mrs Salt's next two words.

'Darren Fisher.'

Tom rocked. Not Darren – Darren the brick shed, the Year Six champion crisp eater, pop guzzler and official tough guy. It wasn't possible. Darren didn't do games. He was always out of breath. Your only defence was to run away from Darren, which worked,

70

and hope that he'd forget your crime against him, which didn't. The thought of having Darren Fisher in his team was just too horrible to contemplate.

'Well?' said Mrs Salt.

'Er . . . er . . . er,' said Tom.

'I can see why you'd be surprised, Tom, but the bottom line is that I think it would do our Darren good to be part of a team. He needs to learn about working with others. And he's very keen. He told me so himself.'

'Darren? Keen? To play football?'

'Yes. So that's agreed then, is it?' said Mrs Salt, rising to her feet and smiling. Tom had forgotten the third smile, the one that meant, 'This is how it's going to be, so don't even bother to argue.'

'Yes, Mrs Salt,' he said. 'That's fine.'

It was break time. Tom began to search for the other Sharpshooters to tell them about their new signing. As he did so, he tried hard to imagine Darren Fisher carrying out a simple command like 'Pass it, Daz,' or 'Leave it, my ball, Daz.' He just wouldn't do it. Nobody ever told Darren what to do. All Tom could see was disaster after disaster as Darren blundered around the pitch, hoofing away at the ball and shoving everybody else around. He might get sent off, thought Tom, and then they'd be down to four players. The whole situation was so crazy that Tom had to stop and rub his eyes.

At that moment Darren came up and gave him a friendly shove in the back that sent him flying.

'Now then, Skipper,' laughed Darren, 'did old Salt and Vinegar have a word?'

Tom, still winded, nodded.

'Good. You see,' Darren continued in a crumbly way

for he was deep at work with a bag of crisps, 'my dad told me last night that if I ever played football anything like as good as George Best does on this video he's got, he'd take me to Florida. Said that last night to his mate Brian. So I thought, easy, I'll join old Tom Bell's team, he needs a star player. And that's me.'

Tom nodded again. 'Fine,' he smiled.

At that moment Mr Jardine walked past and Darren called out to him, 'Hey, sir, was George Best good or what, sir?'

The teacher's expression softened as his eyes filled with a faraway look. 'George Best, lad, was a genius. An exciting, gifted player of great skill and courage.'

'There you are then,' Darren said after the teacher had moved on. 'Great skill and courage. That's me all right. Isn't it?'

Tom nodded.

Tom called for a practice in the park on Saturday morning. Darren was late. As the others peppered Craig with shots, some of which he saved, Tom began to worry. They had little chance against Dixon's Dynamos as it was, but at least if Darren turned up Tom could try and talk some tactics to him.

At last he did roll up, Coke can in one hand and crisps in the other.

'Overslept,' he muttered. 'Here, kick us the ball.'

Kerry obliged, and all the team waited with interest to see just what Darren would do.

Darren usually didn't bother much with PE. Any unwise laughter at his large frame wobbling round the hall was met with uncompromising physical attack, and as for Games, he developed chronic asthma at frequent intervals. But now he wanted to be George Best. He wanted to be graceful and athletic. He wanted to create magic with a football.

Staring Craig smack in the eye, Darren said, 'Taking a penalty, Wardy, OK?' He placed the ball with ponderous care and slowly marched away for several paces. Turning, he shouted, 'Georgie Best did this,' lowered his head and ran at the ball like an angry rhino. He reached the ball, raised his leg for an almighty blow to slam Craig through the goal and into the wall beyond, and fell over. The ball, caught by his flailing leg, trickled towards the corner flag.

Tom groaned, Kerry dared to laugh, Craig ran to get the ball, Gurteak grinned quietly and Darren swore. He got up and glared at Kerry. 'Giz that ball.'

Once again he carefully placed the ball, his tongue sticking out and his breathing forced. Once again he walked stiffly away, turned and charged the ball, head down like an even angrier rhino with a head cold. Once again he fell over. This time the ball skewed off his foot so badly that it went backwards. Darren got up and stared hard at Tom. 'Your ball's rubbish, Belly,' he said. 'Won't stay still. Is it flat or what?' Tom groaned again.

On his third try, Darren did make contact with the ball and it flew towards the tree tops like a fat, round blackbird, then dipped and whistled towards the top corner of the goal. Darren threw wide his arms to celebrate, but Craig jumped and neatly headed the ball over the bar. 'No goal!' he cried in triumph. 'Aaagh! Dazzer! Get off!'

They all pulled Darren off the flattened goalkeeper and began to explain that landing on the goalie feet first and trying to pull his arms out of their sockets wasn't allowed, but all Darren could say was, 'It were a goal that, cheats.'

*

That afternoon, in his garden, Tom began to talk tactics. Darren slept on the lawn in the afternoon sunshine as Sam and Emma, Tom's little brother and sister, played in their paddling pool. Kerry gave Darren a dig in the ribs with her foot and that brought him to life, grunting and wanting to know how it was a daft girl was playing in their team anyway.

Gurteak explained it was only fair but doubted that Darren heard him. Craig explained that Kerry was really hot stuff with a ball. Tom explained that Craig was right and Kerry explained by keeping her football in the air for twenty kicks, flicking it from left foot to right, knocking it into Darren's stomach and neatly trapping the return. He lay back in the grass, winded, and went to sleep until Emma tipped her dinosaur bucket full of water over his face.

The tactics talk did not amount to much. All Tom could offer in the way of coaching was to tell his team to cling on until the end and hope that they'd win on penalties.

'You stay back with me in midfield, Kerry,' he said. 'Gurteak can do the goal scoring and Daz can be full back, in the heart of our defence,' he added to encourage a frowning Darren.

'Hold on a minute,' Darren said. 'Heart of the defence? What do you mean, heart of the defence? George Best wasn't the heart of the defence.'

'He was when he had to be,' said Kerry. 'Honest.'

'In there like a steam train,' agreed Gurteak. 'Really.'

'Don't give me that!' he growled. 'I've seen him on my dad's videos. One hundred best goals with that bloke off the telly, Cheery Keery, you know? That daft nerd with the silly voices and exploding settees.'

Tom nodded. They'd all seen Cheery Keery's television show full of wacky japes and unfunny pets singing songs.

'Well, on that video George Best does all the goal scoring, not the defending. He's the star and I'm being him. Right?'

There was no arguing with that.

On Sunday afternoon they met up in the park again for a final practice.

'Right, you lot,' said Tom briskly. 'Last chance to practise before the big match.'

For over an hour four of the Sharpshooters kicked, flicked, trapped, slammed and booted the ball. They worked out a free kick tactic, which involved Gurteak receiving a flick over the defender's head from Tom and whacking in a low shot to the corner.

'Old Jardine doesn't worry about any height rules so it might just work,' said Tom and they all agreed.

They talked defence and the need to keep out of the goalie's area, and they talked about keeping up their spirits against tough opposition. Craig dived and leapt. They ended up red faced, sweating and out of breath.

All this time Darren contented himself with a less demanding training programme. It largely consisted of sitting next to the pitch and chewing a blade of grass, although every now and then he threw in a variation and lay down to stretch like a cat in the sun.

Eventually, Tom had had enough. 'Now look, Darren,' he said. 'You ought to do some training.'

'I have, mate, I've trained hard.'

'What?'

'Last night, Smelly Belly, I put some work in, I can tell you.'

'How d'you mean?'

Darren, with something like enthusiasm, got to his

feet. 'I watched all my Dad's Cheery Keery videos about George Best. So now I know all his moves – how he wiggles past those full-backs, how he leaps when he scores a goal, how he pulls his shirt out of his shorts. I've got it all worked out now.'

'That's training, is it, Daz?' Tom asked in disbelief.

'Oh yeh,' Darren said, starting to leave. 'And anyway . . .' he turned round to look at all four of his team mates and smiled a long, slow, Darren Fisher smile, 'anyone who tries to beat me, I'll kill them.'

'I hope he's joking,' said Kerry as the large figure shambled away.

'Course he is,' said Tom. 'Mrs Salt will watch him like a hawk.'

'He'll get us all done,' grumbled Craig. 'As if we haven't enough on with Dixon and his Dynamos.'

In the event, their worries came to nothing. Darren seemed in an unusually sunny mood on Monday. Of course, before school and during break time in the morning, everyone was talking about the lunchtime match. Each time someone mentioned it Tom felt his stomach tweak another notch like a guitar being over-tuned. Through all this tension, plus the added difficulty of Mr Jardine choosing this of all mornings to introduce a particularly unpleasant and stubborn type of decimal fraction to Y6J, Darren remained the calmest of all the Sharpshooters. He was even well behaved during lunchtime and enjoyed his meal noisily, despite all the other four team members tasting nothing but ashes and charcoal.

As they got changed for the game, Darren whispered to Tom, 'Don't worry, skipper, I saw that vid again last night. I've got my moves worked out OK.'

Tom tried to smile, his cardboard dinner churning

in his stomach. 'Great, Daz,' he said. 'You keep it flowing.'

The weather was warm, with a slight breeze. Ideal. As Tom led his team onto the field, he looked around. The whole school seemed to be surrounding the pitch. He could see Mrs Salt and several of the other teachers amongst the crowd, and there was Mr Jardine in his tracksuit and gleaming white trainers, whistle, stop-watch, pencil and notebook all ready to start. As Dixon's Dynamos joined them on the field the whole crowd roared their excitement, and Luke felt all his tension and nervousness slip away. Even the sight of Lee and Robert doing some flashy ball-juggling as they warmed up didn't worry him.

He looked at his team. Gurteak was a match for anyone, slippery and sharp in attack and a tiger in defence. Kerry was dependable, with good skills. Craig, looking pale, would be fine once he got his first save of the match under his belt. Tom felt that he could probably handle midfield although Lee was sometimes too strong for him, and Robert could dazzle you with his footwork. Then there was Darren. He had some old blue shorts on that looked too small, over which he pulled down his red shirt. He was beaming around at the crowd, enjoying the atmos-phere. He was big, strong and solid-looking. If he would just stay in defence and keep out of Wardy's area they might have a chance.

From the moment the Dynamos kicked off, things moved quickly. To Tom, it was a blur of feet skipping past him, the ball whizzing into empty spaces danger-ously near Craig's goal, the voices of Lee and Robert controlling the movement of the ball as they hit passes to each other with fierce precision. A moment of danger when Craig fumbled a shot from Tracy Hardwick; another of joy when he punched away a real scorcher from Joe Spenser. A moment of brilliance from Gurteak which nearly put them in the lead. A moment of near despair when Darren stuck out a leg where the ball might have been once in its life but not then, flooring Lee who then saw his free kick scream over the crossbar leaving Craig wrong-footed and open mouthed. Four minutes into the game, things settled to a more obvious pattern with the Dynamos attacking almost continuously, the Sharpshooters defending as best they could, and Darren getting in everybody's way.

Then Robert Dixon scored.

All around him Tom could see the crowd cheering and yelling, and he felt his energy punched out of him like air from a punctured tyre. Craig pulled the ball out of the net and rolled it to him. Kerry smiled, Gurteak shrugged and Darren came over and said, 'I've still got those moves ready, skipper, don't you worry.' Before Tom could think of what to say, Mr Jardine blew for half-time.

As they changed ends Tom shouted, 'Come on, you Sharpshooters! We can do it!' and immediately felt better when he heard a voice yell, 'It's not over yet, Tom!' Other parts of the crowd joined in, lifting the team's spirits. However, as soon as the whistle blew two things happened almost at once. The first was that the Dynamos swept down on the Sharpshooters and pinned them into defence, and the second was that Darren Fisher began to show off his moves. As the game took up most of one half of the pitch, he concentrated on the other and began to run, jink and skip around imaginary defenders with only Dekko as an audience. To begin with Dekko was amused, but then as Kerry lobbed a rare attacking ball in his direction, he got irritated and complained that Darren was in his way and putting him off on purpose.

'He keeps dancing about in front of me, ref,' Dekko complained. 'Trying to make me laugh and that. It's not fair.'

'I'm only doing my moves,' grumbled Darren. 'Never seen George Best before?'

The Dynamos were awarded a free kick and Darren began to sulk.

Robert took the kick but it flew over the bar. Craig quickly rolled the ball out to Tom. He looked up and saw Gurteak free and wide. Sidestepping Lee, Tom brought the ball into the midfield, intending to sweep it out to Gurteak on the wing. Before he could, Robert came thundering in and took his legs away from his body. As he floated in mid-air Tom thought, 'That was a foul.' He thudded into the grass, winded and feeling sore, but the whistle had gone and they had a free kick near Dekko's goal.

'You OK, Tommy?' asked Mr Jardine.

'Fine,' gasped Tom.

'One more of those, Robert, and you're off. This isn't the World Cup, you know.'

'No, Mr Jardine. Sorry, Tom.'

Tom knew how much all this meant to Robert. He straightened up over the ball and looked at the crowd, quietened by this dramatic moment, and he knew it was important for him as well. Gurteak stared at him and winked. They had to try it, thought Tom. It must be nearly full-time. Now or never.

The whistle blew and Tom carefully put his right foot under the curve of the ball. It had worked twice in the park. Go for it.

He saw the ball, almost in slow motion, loop high

79

over the Dynamos' wall. It bounced once in the empty space between them and the goal, and then Gurteak pounced. With one crisp movement he had controlled the ball, turned his body and delivered a shot that left Dekko face down in the mud and the ball rammed into the back of the goal. They had equalized.

The roar from the spectators almost knocked Tom over. It was like a warm blast that shoved him in the chest. The Dynamos looked sick, and the Sharp-shooters were jumping and shouting like mad things. Apart from Darren, that is. Having been told not to do his moves by the referee he was still in a state of great sulk. As the match restarted, he deliberately wandered over to the wing near Dekko's goal, already a long way from the action, and began talking to Luke Fletcher who was on the front row chewing some mints.

Tom, scrambling in defence, was hoping for the final whistle and penalties. He hardly missed his fifth team-mate but, looking up, happened to see that Darren was free and on the wing. He seemed to be talking to someone in the crowd, but as the ball rolled free for a second, Tom whacked it upfield and shouted, 'Daz, Shoot!'

Darren hardly looked up. He had lost all interest in the game, which seemed to him like any other game; a lot of fuss and bother and hard work for nothing. Getting mints off Luke Fletcher would be much easier and far more rewarding. When the football that he was supposed to be kicking passed by him and out of play, he hardly saw it. When Dekko placed it in the area, hoping for one last boot down at the Sharp-shooters' net in the dying seconds of the game, Darren could not have cared less.

Luke, for once escaping the eagle glare of Mrs Salt,

had thrown Darren his tube of mints and Darren, of course, had missed them. They lay in the middle of the field, quite near the edge of Dekko's area. Darren was after those mints in a moment. Thoughts of football now vanished. He had, he reasoned, literally tried his best. Far from being applauded as a wizard of the wing, he had been ridiculed and forced to give away a free kick. Football, he concluded as he bent to pick up the sweets with his back to Dekko's goal, was daft. Total rubbish.

At that moment Dekko unleashed his giant kick. The ball flew from his foot like a rocket and slammed into Darren's broad backside, making him shoot forwards and miss the mints. The ball rebounded with incredible energy right into Dekko's empty goal. Mr Jardine blew for time and the Sharpshooters had won.

At the other end, Tommy, who had seen Darren ignore his upfield ball, felt his anger turn to incredible happiness. Amongst all the howls of laughter and the cheering and whooping he raced up to Darren who was slowly getting to his feet. 'Daz! Daz!' he shouted. 'You scored! We've won!'

Darren looked at his captain and silently offered him a rather grubby mint. 'Told you my moves would work, didn't I?'

'Does this mean you go to Florida, Darren?'

Tom received a stone-cold stare. 'No. It was a joke.'

'Oh,' said Tom. 'I'm sorry, Daz.'

'S'all right. He said if we won the competition he'd give me a quid.'

'We're playing Jacko's Giants or Barry's Blades now. I don't think we'll beat either of them.'

'Maybe not.' Darren grinned. 'Just depends on whose videos I decide to look at next, doesn't it?'

Simon Comes Home

Redvers Brandling

'Come on, Cranfield. Three minutes to go.'

The players were tired. It had been a long hard match played in thick mud. Now, as darkness closed in, a steady rain began to fall. Standing near the centre circle with his red and white striped shirt plastered to him, Simon's feet felt cold and wet. The score was still 0–0 and it seemed like three weeks since he had touched the ball.

He stood there watching play at the other end of the field when suddenly Winston Worrell, Cranfield's best defender, got the ball. Instead of booting it upfield he put his head down and began to run. Galloping and splashing through the mud, he came up the right wing like a runaway tank. Turning quickly, Simon began to run with him in the centre of the field.

'Get back!'

'Watch the wing.'

'Mark the centre!'

There were shouts of panic from the Belton defence – and yells of encouragement from the Cranfield fans.

Winston didn't seem to hear any of it. Lunging towards the right corner flag he left two Belton players trailing behind him. Simon was near the penalty spot, with bodies all round him, when Winston lashed the ball across. What happened next was amazing.

The ball hurtled across the goal at waist height.

Before Simon could reach it, the blue and white stock-inged leg of a defender deflected it high, hard and goalwards. The goalkeeper, who had come rushing out, stood dumbfounded as the ball rocketed over his shoulder.

Bang!

It rattled the crossbar and bounced back towards the tangled mass of players. Hitting the still onrushing Simon on the knee it fizzed into the back of the net before anybody else could move.

Goal! He'd actually scored a goal!

Two minutes to go and the weary Belton team knew it really was all over. The Cranfield fans were sure too.

'What a team!'

'Yeah, yeah, *yeah*!'

'Cran . . . *field*.'

Cheer after cheer refused to be muffled by the rain – and then the piercing blast of the referee's whistle signalled the end.

Cranfield's sports teacher, Mr Richards, known to everybody as 'Old Dick', stood on the touchline as the teams ran off.

'Well done, everybody,' he called to both teams, and then, clapping his hands, he called his own team round him.

'Good work, Winston; well played, Leroy.'

He had a word for everybody, and then gave Simon a friendly punch on the arm.

'The winner, eh, Simon?'

Then, raising his voice, he spoke to the whole group.

'Right, hurry up, Cranfield. Changed and in the minibus to go back to school in twenty minutes. Come on, chop-chop!'

As the team got changed amidst an excited chatter, Simon stood quietly, away from the others. Pulling off his boots, the same old mixed feeling swept over him. Oh yes, he'd scored the winner but he, and everyone else, knew it was a fluke. Anyway, nobody wanted to share the moment with him – except Old Dick, of course.

One or two of the other kids spoke to him from time to time if they had to, but he still felt an outsider. That's what he'd been from the moment he'd come to this school.

It had been just over five weeks ago, on a cold, misty January morning . . .

'Come in, Mrs Morley,' the head teacher had said to Simon's mum.

Simon just sat there while they talked.

'What a dump,' he thought to himself. 'Never be as good as Minley here . . . never.'

But his father had lost his job, then got another one in Cranfield so they'd had to move. He'd never like it though. He just knew it.

'Simon.'

Simon jumped as the head teacher spoke to him.

'So, you've come from Minley. Famous for its football team, eh? I'm sure you're a good footballer then!'

Simon opened his mouth to say that he wasn't, but the head teacher was already turning away. Putting her hand on his mother's shoulder she moved to the door.

'Perhaps you'd like to come with Simon to his new class, Mrs Morley.'

And that's how it had all started. When he got to the classroom the head teacher introduced him and his mother to Mr Richards, the class teacher, and then started on about the 'good footballer' bit all over again. Naturally the kids in the class were all ears.

Well, Simon wasn't a good footballer and that's all there was to it. He was dead keen, of course, but on the pitch he was dead clumsy too. Naturally the other kids soon found this out, but Cranfield was a very small school, so whenever Harry Wagstaffe couldn't play, Simon was in the school team. He was the substitute striker.

Harry Wagstaffe – everybody called him 'Waggy' – was Simon's main problem. Waggy was cheerfully cheeky and a great footballer. He was popular with every kid in the school. When he found out that Simon was supposed to be a good footballer – and wasn't – there was trouble.

'Good?' sneered Waggy in the playground. 'Who said you were good?'

'It wasn't me . . .' Simon began.

It was no use. Waggy had already turned scornfully away.

Something else also annoyed Waggy. Simon had a 'fly-paper' memory. Facts and figures stuck in his mind like flies to sticky paper. This meant he could give Mr Richards all the right answers in class.

'You think you're clever, don't you?' Waggy poked Simon with a finger.

'No! Things just sort of stick in my head – don't know why.' Simon tried to be friendly, but it wasn't any good.

Waggy drop-kicked the tennis ball he'd been holding and put his face close to Simon's.

'We don't like show-offs here. Old Dick might like you, but *we don't*!'

Without another word he swirled round and ran after the tennis ball. Cheering and yelling his gang followed him up the playground. Simon was left by himself.

From then on it got worse. If Waggy didn't like you it seemed no one else would. Even Mehnaz, the kindest girl in the class, hardly said a friendly word. Simon was always picked last for any team game, no one would make a 'pair' with him in PE, his pencil points got mysteriously broken, his jacket always managed to be 'accidentally' knocked onto the floor of the cloakroom. Every breaktime he was by himself. It was no fun. Simon hated it.

Suddenly Simon's thoughts were brought back to the present. Mr Richards was shouting again.

'Five minutes and we're off. *Hurry up*. Ah . . . and while I remember, there's a football meeting for every-body tomorrow. Breaktime in my classroom.'

As Simon picked up his boots, he heard Ivor Bork speak to Winston Worrell.

'Bet we'd have scored more if Waggy had been playing.'

'Yeah, no problem.'

Waggy had been absent with a cold.

At breaktime next morning Mr Richards' room was full. All the team members were there – a lot of the girl players too. Then there were the supporters, and even Mrs Leach the head teacher. She pushed her hair back and spoke first.

'Mr Richards has told me about last night. Very well done, all of you. Now Mr Richards has got some rather special news.'

'Right,' said Old Dick. He always started his football talks off by saying 'Right.'

'Right – now, how about this for exciting news. Last night was, of course, the quarter final of the Murray

Cup. On Thursday night it's the semi-final against Granby School. And . . .'

Mr Richards paused and rubbed his hands. Then he went on.

'And . . . if we win, the final will be played at Rokeby Park!'

'Cor!'

'Wow!'

There were gasps of excitement. Rokeby Park was the home of Newlands United, well on course to becoming champions of the Endsleigh League, Division 1. There were grandstands, and changing rooms, and dugouts. Fancy Cranfield playing there!

'Fantastic!' shouted Winston Worrell.

Everybody agreed with him.

'But . . .' went on Dick Richards, ' . . . do please quieten down . . . But, first of all we've got to beat Granby. And that won't be easy. Now, I'll collect the shirts from last night's game.'

Ivor collected the shirts their mothers had washed.

'By the way,' said Mr, Richards, 'I haven't had your shirt, Harry Wagstaffe, and that's from two matches ago.'

Waggy was back from his cold. Naturally he had forgotten his shirt. He forgot everything.

'Sorry, sir. I'll bring it tomorrow.'

'You'd better. You'd forget your false teeth if you had any.'

There was a bit of a snigger at this, and then Old Dick held up his hand.

'Right – team for the Granby match.'

Everybody listened as eleven names were read out. Waggy was back so Simon was not in the eleven, but he was a substitute.

Even though Simon wasn't in the team, he prepared

as if he was going to play for Manchester United at Wembley. He cleaned his boots three times, did press-ups before going to bed, press-ups when he got up, deep-breathing exercises at his open bedroom window.

And then . . . it was the day of the semi-final.

The game was on a secondary school field. There was a big crowd there – children, teachers, mums and dads – ready to cheer both teams as they ran onto the pitch. Simon stood in his strip and anorak next to the other substitutes.

When the match got started, everybody knew it was going to be a hard game. Granby were a big brawny lot and their all-white strip made them seem even bigger. Having won the toss they chose to kick with the strong wind which was blowing, and right from the kick-off they put the pressure on the Cranfield defence.

There were three corners in the first ten minutes and from each one Cranfield goalie Nicky Obago had to make a save. But, well as the Cranfield defenders played, the undoubted star was Waggy. He was everywhere – tackling on the wings, clearing up the middle, and even on one occasion heading a long-range shot off the line.

'That's some player you've got there,' muttered the Granby coach to Mr Richards.

'You ain't seen nothin' yet!' smiled Dick in reply. 'Wait till the second half.'

When the half-time whistle blew, Dick gathered the team around him.

'Well done, lads,' he said. 'That was a good job done keeping them out in this wind. It'll be helping you this half so try and make the most of it.'

'You bet, sir,' chirped Waggy. Despite all the chasing about he'd done, his face was one big grin and he looked as fit as a fiddle. 'Now it's our turn to make them suffer.'

Going round with a plastic sack to collect the orange squash beakers, Simon could tell that the team was confident. When the ref's whistle summoned them back on the field they could hardly wait for the kick-off.

Now, with the wind blowing even more strongly than before, it was a very different match. Cranfield, in their red and white striped shirts and black shorts, pushed forward continually into the Granby half. Nicky Obago was a shivering spectator at the other end.

But now there were two stars on the pitch. Waggy was as brilliant as ever – this time as an attacker – but the big ginger-haired Granby goalkeeper played like a man inspired. Shots poured in on him – long-rangers from Winston and Borky, flicks, lobs and headers from Waggy and the other forwards. It made no difference. He caught them or punched them or kicked them, but none got past him.

Standing next to Mr Richards, Simon could sense he was getting frustrated. It seemed that Cranfield would never score, but one player kept going as if he had no doubts whatsoever. Grinning, shouting, encouraging, Waggy ranged across the pitch like a red and white shirted terrier.

Then, with about quarter of an hour to go, he picked up a stray ball on the halfway line. Trapping it and turning in one smooth movement he shouted, 'Wing, Winston', pointed with his right hand and then floated a well-weighted chip up towards the corner flag.

Winston Worrell was already after it. Side by side with a Granby defender he managed to reach the ball a fraction ahead of his opponent. Without hesitation he crashed it into the centre in his usual style.

Waggy was waiting. As the ball reached him he bent his knees and gently headed it over the defender who was marking him. Then, rounding him like lightning, he crashed a fierce volley high into the roof of the net.

'Waggy . . . Waggy . . . *Waggy!*' the Cranfield fans chanted.

Waggy gave them a thumbs-up as he ran back to the centre.

Granby knew that time was running out. Full of spirit and determination, and despite the wind, they forced Cranfield back again. Ginger, Granby's goalie, bellowed encouragement to the players in front of him.

After ten minutes of intense Granby pressure, Cranfield broke away again. Swarming upfield they were only denied a second goal by a last-minute sliding tackle from one of Granby's central defenders.

Corner!

Winston came up to take it as usual. The goalmouth was like rush hour in a big city, bodies pushing and jostling everywhere.

'Come on, come on, mark everybody,' called Ginger anxiously.

Out at the corner flag, Winston measured his run-up. Smack! Over came the ball, twisting and dipping in the wind.

'Mine!' yelled Ginger, rushing out of his goal. But it wasn't.

As the tall goalie lunged for the ball a sudden gust of wind lifted it over his outstretched fingers. And there waiting, as if he had known this was exactly what would happen, was Waggy. A quick flick of his head – and the ball was in the back of the net.

'*Goal!*'

'*Cranfield for ever!*'

Now there were only five minutes to go. Dick Richards turned to the three subs.

'Right lads. Anoraks off. On you go.'

Waggy was one of the players substituted. He gave a friendly punch to Ade and Billy as they went on. He ignored Simon.

In the last five minutes Simon touched the ball twice. He slipped on it and gave Granby a throw-in, and he headed against the back of one of his own players. Still, when the final whistle went, he was as excited as anybody. Cranfield were going to play at Rokeby Park!

The final was due to be played in a fortnight's time, and that meant there was plenty of opportunity for Waggy to get on Mr Richards' nerves in the classroom. Every day there was something.

'Harry Wagstaffe – where's your maths book?'

'Dunno, sir.'

'What do you mean, you've lost your pen?'

'Dunno sir – just lost it.'

'Who left that mess in the library corner?'

'Waggy, sir.'

But it was in an unforgettable PE lesson when the accident happened. The best four gymnasts in the class were doing handsprings over the vaulting horse and Mr Richards was standing by, supervizing things carefully. Naturally Waggy was one of the stars and after one spectacular leap and landing he let out a great shout of 'Yeah!'

Old Dick half turned in irritation – and that was the moment Melanie Ashley's hand slipped off the vaulting horse, and she toppled sideways into the teacher. He had of course been standing by for just this sort of thing but, momentarily distracted by Waggy's shout, he was off balance when Melanie hit him. Cushioning her fall expertly he took her weight, but couldn't stay upright. With a flurry of arms and legs girl and teacher hit the hall floor. Melanie was up in a flash.

'Sorry, sir. Thanks for catching me, sir . . . sir?'

Mr Richards lay on the floor. His face was pale and he clutched his left ankle.

'Melanie,' he said, in a shaky voice, 'you and Ceri go and get Mr Beveridge. Tell him I need a bit of help.'

In a minute Mr Beveridge, another teacher on the staff, had arrived. Old Greeny, the caretaker, came with him. Between them they lifted Mr Richards up and carried him off in the direction of the staffroom. Mrs Leach was now in the hall too and she lined up the class and took them back to the classroom.

Next day there was a supply teacher, and news of old Dick. He had a badly sprained ankle and wouldn't be back for over a week.

'Mr Richards should be back just before the big match at Rokeby,' Mrs Leach told the class.

The week that Dick was away was a strange one. The supply teacher was OK – not as good as Dick, but OK. Usually new teachers had a hard time with Waggy and he gave them non-stop trouble. Not this time though. He was so quiet you hardly noticed him.

Then there was the night Simon saw him training. Riding his bike near Marley's Field, Simon saw Waggy and his big brother, Wayne. Wayne was throwing a football to Waggy who was flicking it from one foot to another and then shooting back. This was the sort of stuff Waggy usually couldn't be bothered with.

Next day, Simon heard Waggy and Ivor talking in the dinner line.

'Soon be the big match, Wag.'

'Yeah.'

'What's the matter? Aren't you looking forward to it?'

''Course I am. It's just that . . .'

'What?'

'Well – we've *got* to win. That's what.'

'Yeah, but—'

'Oh shut up, will you!'

As Simon listened, he suddenly remembered Waggy's face when Mr Richards had been carried from the hall. It had been pale and worried. He knew the accident had been partly his fault. And Simon now knew why Waggy was so obviously desperate for Cranfield to win the match. He had to put things right – prove to the teacher that he really was sorry for messing everything up. If they lost because Mr Richards hadn't been around for training, then Waggy would feel it was all his fault.

Big match day! The final at last! School was closed half an hour early so that everybody could get to Rokeby Park for the four o'clock kick-off. Everybody was excited – even Mrs Leach was wearing a red and white scarf, and Jasmin had brought a huge teddy bear and dressed it in a spare Cranfield shirt – the team even had a mascot!

The team and substitutes left early and were soon at the ground. They were going to get changed in Newlands United's dressing room.

Mr Richards hobbled in, leaning heavily on a walking stick.

'Right,' he said. 'Now listen carefully.'

The players all stopped what they were doing.

'Right – now here we are at Rokeby Park, and the main thing is for everybody to enjoy the experience. But, we want to beat Borrowdale and they are a very good team. So – try hard not to make any early mis-takes and don't give any daft goals away. Then . . .'

Suddenly Mr Richards stopped.

'Harry Wagstaffe, what is the matter with you, lad?'

'I can't find me boots, sir.'

'What!'

'I know they're somewhere but . . .'

Simon could see that Waggy was close to tears. But Mr Richards had been absent and he'd no idea how upset Waggy had been about the accident. He didn't realize that Waggy wanted to play his best game ever to make up for it.

'Well, let me tell you this,' said the teacher, very, very quietly. 'Unless you find your boots you're not playing. Simon will be striker.'

Simon never knew why he acted as he did at that moment. Somehow it just seemed right.

'Sir!' he called out sharply. 'Waggy asked me to look after his boots for him. Here they are.'

Then Simon handed a plastic bag to an amazed Waggy. In it were Simon's beautifully cleaned boots. He knew Waggy took the same size.

Mr Richards shook his head.

'Thank you, Simon,' he sighed. 'Now, Harry Wag-staffe, get those boots on before you lose them again.'

Waggy still looked amazed. But he put the boots on without a word. Five minutes later the match had begun.

From the start, everything went wrong for Cranfield. After only two minutes there was a terrific goalmouth scramble in front of Nicky Obago. The Cranfield defenders just couldn't get the ball away and when Winston Worrell lunged at it with his weaker left foot, it spun across goal to the prowling Borrowdale striker.

Without a second's hesitation he crashed it wide of Nicky Obago's left hand and into the back of the net.

Half an hour later the fans in green and white were cheering again! This time the goal was due to a mistake by Waggy of all people. Back helping out in defence he tried to dribble clear of danger. Bursting out of the penalty area he suddenly lost control as the ball ran ahead of him. The tall, blond-haired Borrowdale midfielder who had been just about to tackle him decided to try his luck with a shot instead. Whacking the ball clear of Waggy's desperately stretching leg, he grinned with delight as he watched it fizz off the underside of the Cranfield crossbar. Borrowdale 2 Cranfield 0. Luckily there were no more goals before half-time.

When the interval came, nobody could have been kinder or more encouraging than Mr Richards.

'You've made two mistakes, but you're playing really well.'

Then the teacher turned to Waggy.

'But you, Harry, you're trying too hard. You can't be everywhere at once, you know. Just enjoy the game.'

'Yes, sir,' mumbled a pale, quiet Waggy.

The referee's whistle shrilled in the corridor and the team trooped out again. Following them, Simon saw an anorak lying on the floor. He picked it up and there, underneath and tied together with an old lace, were Waggy's battered, patched-up old boots! Putting them under his arm, Simon joined the other subs in the dugout.

The second half had just started when there was a double disaster for Cranfield. Nicky Obago came running out of his goal to collect a high left wing centre. The Borrowdale striker, a constant menace, leapt determindly with him. Between the two, Ivor

Bork, who had been marking the striker throughout, was sandwiched as he made his jump too.

Perhaps put off by his team-mate, Nicky just failed to get his hands to the ball and, with a resounding smack, the striker's forehead powered it into the net.

Goal!

Then, as the Borrowdale players were triumphantly running back to the centre, Ivor Bork tried to get up off the ground – and couldn't. A couple of minutes later he was being helped off the pitch. An awkward fall and a twisted knee meant that he wouldn't be taking any more part in the match.

'Right, Simon,' snapped Mr Richards, 'get on there and play up front with Waggy. We've nothing to lose now and we need goals. Come on, come on – you haven't even got your boots on!'

Lacing up Waggy's boots as fast as he could, Simon stepped onto Rokeby Park.

'Me,' he thought, 'playing at the stadium!'

He gazed up at the grandstands.

'Come on, sunshine,' shouted the linesman, 'you're here to play football. Chop, chop.'

The linesman's shout woke Simon up and, within seconds, he was in action. His first touch of the ball was a surprisingly good one – a shot for the far corner of the goal which the Borrowdale keeper pushed round the post in a swooping dive.

Corner!

Winston came up from the back to take it – and cracked across one of his hard, fast specials. Simon was at the near post and, leaping as high as he could, he just managed to flick it on with his head. The ball flew straight across the face of the goal to the lurking Waggy. Smack! Borrowdale 3 Cranfield 1.

Simon and Waggy ran back to the centre together.

'Good pass, kid,' muttered the scorer.

Simon felt five metres tall – Waggy had spoken to him! And with Waggy's boots on he felt less clumsy than ever before . . . and with Waggy playing beside him . . . well!

For the next half hour, the game surged from one end of the pitch to the other. Both sides attacked flat out. Borrowdale for the killer goal, Cranfield for the one which would give them some hope.

Then . . . a goal kick from Nicky Obago ballooned up to the centre circle and Waggy was onto it in a flash. Now playing with all his old verve and cheek he began dodging and weaving his way upfield. Simon ran beside him, but this time Waggy needed no help. Skipping over one last, desperate tackle he flicked the ball gently out of the goalie's reach. Slowly but surely it rolled into the Borrowdale net.

'Well done Waggy!'

All Cranfield heard Mr Richards' great shout. Could they do it? Five minutes left. One goal to draw . . . two to win.

Borrowdale were rattled. They pulled everybody back to defend. Winston and Leroy came up from the heart of the Cranfield defence and the pressure was really on. Attack followed attack and the fans of both sides were going wild.

Then Waggy got the ball out on the left wing and set off on another of his mazy dribbles. Man after man slid into the tackle and all were left beaten. Reaching the edge of the penalty area Waggy suddenly stopped, paused, and slid the ball perfectly into Simon's path.

With timing he didn't know he had, Simon hit the ball like a rocket and it blurred towards the top corner of the net. A great roar rose from the Cranfield fans.

Then . . . it stopped abruptly. The Borrowdale goalie made a fantastic leap and his straining fingers just managed to touch the ball over the bar. Before the corner could be taken, the final whistle blew.

Borrowdale 3 Cranfield 2.

After that all was excitement. Teams and spectators crowded into the centre of the pitch. Cups and medals were given out and there were gasps of 'wonderful game' from everybody. Mr Richards and Mrs Leach shook all the players' hands.

This time Simon was not alone. As they stood together he felt Waggy's arm round his shoulder.

'Well, we nearly did it, Simon . . . mate.'

The Fib

George Layton

Ooh, I wasn't half snug and warm in bed. I could hear
my mum calling me to get up, but it was ever so cold.
Every time I breathed, I could see a puff of air. The
window was covered with frost. I just couldn't get
myself out of bed.

'Are you up? I've called you three times already.'

'Yes, Mum, of course I am.'

I knew it was a lie, but I just wanted to have a few
more minutes in bed. It was so cosy.

'You'd better be, because I'm not telling you again.'

That was another lie. She was always telling me
again.

'Just you be quick, young man, and frame yourself,
or you'll be late for school.'

Ooh, school! If only I didn't have to go. Thank
goodness we were breaking up soon for Christmas. I
don't mind school, I quite like it sometimes. But today
was Monday, and Mondays was football, and I hate
blooming football. It wouldn't be so bad if I had
proper kit, but I had to play in these old-fashioned
shorts and boots that my mum had got from my Uncle
Kevin. They were huge. Miles too big for me. Gordon
Barraclough's mum and dad had bought him a Bobby
Charlton strip and Bobby Charlton boots. No wonder
he's a better player than me. My mum said she couldn't
see what was wrong with my kit. She couldn't

understand that I felt silly, and all the other lads laughed at me, even Tony, and he's my best friend. She just said she wasn't going to waste good money on new boots and shorts, when I had a perfectly good set already.

'But Mum, they all laugh at me, especially Gordon Barraclough.'

'Well, laugh back at them. You're big enough aren't you? Don't be such a jessie.'

She just couldn't understand.

'You tell them your Uncle Kevin played in those boots when he was a lad, and he scored thousands of goals.'

Blimey, that shows you how old my kit is! My Uncle Kevin's twenty-nine! I snuggled down the bed a bit more, and pulled the pillow under the blankets with me.

'I'm coming upstairs and if I find you not up, there'll be trouble. I'm not telling you again.'

Oh heck! I forced myself out of bed on to the freezing lino and got into my underpants. Ooh, they were cold! Blooming daft this. Getting dressed, going to school, and getting undressed again to play rotten football. I looked out of the window and it didn't half look miserable. I *felt* miserable. I *was* miserable. Another ninety minutes standing between the posts, letting in goal after goal, with Gordon Barraclough shouting at me:

'Why didn't you dive for it, you lazy beggar?'

Why didn't *he* dive for it? Why didn't *he* go in goal? Why didn't he shut his rotten mouth? Oh no, *he* was always centre forward wasn't he, because *he* was Bobby Charlton.

As I stood looking out of the window, I started wondering how I could get out of going to football . . . I know, I'd tell my mum I wasn't feeling well. I'd tell her I'd got a cold. No, a sore throat. No, she'd look. Swollen glands. Yes, that's what I'd tell her, swollen glands. No, she'd feel. What could I say was wrong with me? Earache, yes, earache, and I'd ask her to write me a note. I'd ask her after breakfast. Well, it was only a fib, wasn't it?

'You're very quiet. Didn't you enjoy your breakfast?'

'Err . . . well . . . I don't feel very well, Mum. I think I've got earache.'

'You *think* you've got earache?'

'I mean I *have* got earache, definitely, in my ear.'

'Which ear?'

'What?'

'You going deaf as well? I said, which ear?'

'Err . . . my right ear. Perhaps you'd better write me a note to get me off football . . .'

'No, love, it'll be good for you to go to football, get some fresh air. I'll write to Mr Melrose and ask him to let you go in goal, so you don't have to run around too much.'

She'd write a note to *ask* if I could go in . . .! Melrose didn't need a note for me to go in goal. I was *always* shoved in goal. Me and Norbert Lightowler were always in goal, because we were the worst players.

Norbert didn't care. He was never bothered when people shouted at him. He just told them to get lost. He never even changed for football. He just stuffed his trousers into his socks and said it was a tracksuit. He nearly looked as daft as me in my Uncle Kevin's old kit.

'Mum, don't bother writing me a note. I'll be all right.'

'I'm only thinking of you. If you've got earache I don't want you to run around too much. I don't want you in bed for Christmas.'

'I'll be OK.'

Do you know, I don't think my mum believed I'd got earache. I know I was fibbing, but even if I had got earache, I don't think she'd have believed me. Mums are like that.

'Are you sure you're all right?'

'Yes, I'll be OK.'

How could my mum know that when I was in goal I ran around twice as much, anyway? Every time the other team scored, I had to belt halfway across the playing field to fetch the ball back.

'Well, finish your Rice Krispies. Tony'll be here in a minute.'

Tony called for me every morning. I was never ready. I was just finishing my toast when I heard my mum let him in. He came through to the kitchen.

'Aw, come on. You're never ready.'

'I won't be a minute.'

'We'll be late, we'll miss the football bus.'

We didn't have any playing fields at our school, so we had a special bus to Bankfield Top, about two miles away.

'If we miss the bus, I'll do you.'

'We won't miss the bus. Stop panicking . . .'

I wouldn't have minded missing it.

' . . . anyway we might not have football today. It's very frosty.'

'Course we will. You aren't half soft, you.'

It was all right for Tony, he wasn't bad at football. Nobody shouted at him.

'It's all right for you. Nobody shouts at you.'

'Well, who shouts at you?'

'Gordon Barraclough.'

'You don't want to take any notice. Now hurry up.'

My mum came in with my kit.

'Yes, hurry up or you'll miss your bus for football.'

'We won't miss our rotten bus for rotten football.'

She gave me a clout on the back of my head. Tony laughed.

'And you can stop laughing, Tony Wainwright,' and she gave him a clout, as well. 'Now go on, both of you.'

We ran to school and got there in plenty of time. I knew we would.

Everybody was getting on the bus. We didn't have to go to assembly when it was football. Gordon Barraclough was on the top deck with his head out of the window. He saw me coming.

'Hey, Gordon Banks . . .'

He always called me that, because he thinks Gordon Banks was the best goalie ever. He reckons he was called Gordon after Gordon Banks.

'Hey, Gordon Banks, how many goals are you going to let in today?'

Tony nudged me.

'Don't take any notice.'

'Come on, Gordon Banks, how many goals am I going to get against you . . .?'

Tony nudged me again.

'Ignore him.'

' . . . or am I going to be lumbered with you on my side, eh?'

'He's only egging you on. Ignore him.'

Yes, I'll ignore him. That's the best thing. I'll ignore him.

'If you're on my side, Gordon Banks, you'd better not let any goals in, or I'll do you.'

Just ignore him, that's the best thing.

'Get lost, Barraclough, you rotten big-head.'

I couldn't ignore him. Tony was shaking his head.

'I told you to ignore him.'

'I couldn't.'

Gordon still had his head out of the window.

'I'm coming down to get you.'

And he would've done, too, if it hadn't been for Norbert. Just as Gordon was going back into the bus, Norbert wound the window up, so Gordon's head was stuck. It must've hurt him, well, it could have choked him.

'You're a maniac, Lightowler. You could have choked me.'

Norbert just laughed, and Gordon thumped him, right in the neck, and they started fighting. Tony and me ran up the stairs to watch. They were rolling in the aisle. Norbert got on top of Gordon and put his knees on his shoulders. Everybody was watching now, and shouting:

'Fight! Fight! Fight! Fight!'

The bell hadn't gone for assembly yet, and other lads from the playground came out to watch.

'Fight! Fight! Fight! Fight!'

Gordon pushed Norbert off him, and they rolled under a seat. Then they rolled out into the aisle again, only this time Gordon was on top. He thumped Norbert right in the middle of his chest. Hard. It hurt him, and Norbert got his mad up. I really wanted him to do Gordon.

'Go on, Norbert, do him.'

Just then, somebody clouted me on the back of my head, right where my mum had hit me that morning. I turned round to belt whoever it was.

'Who do you think you're thumping...? Oh, morning, Mr Melrose.'

He pushed me away, and went over to where Norbert and Gordon were still fighting. He grabbed them both by their jackets, and pulled them apart. He used to be in the Commandos, did Mr Melrose.

'Animals! You're a pair of animals! What are you?'

Neither of them said anything. He was still holding them by their jackets. He shook them.

'What are you? Lightowler?'

'A pair of animals.'

'Gordon?'

'A pair of animals, sir. It wasn't my fault, sir. He started it, sir. He wound up that window, sir, and I got my head stuck. He could have choked me, sir.'

Ooh, he was a right tell-tale was Barraclough.

'Why was your head out of the window in the first place?'

'I was just telling someone to hurry up, sir.'

He's a liar as well, but he knew he was all right with Melrose, because he's his favourite.

'And then Lightowler wound up the window, for no reason, sir. He could've choked me.'

Melrose didn't say anything. He just looked at Norbert. Norbert looked back at him with a sort of smile on his face. I don't think he meant to be smiling. It was because he was nervous.

'I'm sick of you, Lightowler, do you know that? I'm sick and tired of you. You're nothing but a trouble-maker.'

Norbert didn't say anything. His face just twitched a bit. It was dead quiet on the bus. The bell went for assembly and we could hear the other classes filing into school.

'A trouble-maker and a hooligan. You're a disgrace to the school, do you know that, Lightowler?'

'Yes, sir.'

'I can't wait for the day you leave, Lightowler.'

'Neither can I, sir.'

Melrose's hand moved so fast that it made *everybody* jump, not just Norbert. It caught him right on the side of his face. His face started going red straight away. Poor old Norbert. I didn't half feel sorry for him. It wasn't fair. He was helping me.

'Sir, can I . . .?'

'Shut up!'

Melrose didn't even turn round, and I didn't need telling twice. I shut up. Norbert's cheek was getting redder. He didn't rub it though, and it must've been stinging like anything. He's tough, is Norbert.

'You're a lout, Lightowler. What are you?'

'A lout, sir.'

'You haven't even got the decency to wear a school blazer.'

Norbert was wearing a grey jacket that was miles too big for him. He didn't have a school blazer.

'Aren't you proud of the school blazer?'

'I suppose so.'

'Why don't you wear one, then?'

Norbert rubbed his cheek for the first time.

'I haven't got a school blazer, sir.'

He looked as though he was going to cry.

'My mum can't afford one.'

Nobody moved. Melrose stared at Norbert. It seemed ages before he spoke.

'Get out of my sight, Lightowler. Wait in the classroom until we come back from football. And get your hands out of your pockets. The rest of you sit down and be quiet.'

Melrose went downstairs and told the driver to set off. Tony and me sat on the back seat. As we turned right into Horton Road, I could see Norbert climbing on the school wall, and walking along it like a tightrope walker. Melrose must've seen him as well. He really asks for trouble, does Norbert.

It's about a ten-minute bus ride to Bankfield Top. You go into town, through the City Centre and up Bankfield Road. When we went past the Town Hall, everybody leaned over to look at the Lord Mayor's Christmas tree.

'Back in your seats. You've all seen a Christmas tree before.'

Honestly, Melrose was such a spoil-sport. Course we'd all seen a Christmas tree before, but not as big as that. It must have been about thirty feet tall. There were tons of lights on it as well, *and* there were lights and decorations all round the square and in the shops. Tony said they were being switched on at half past four that afternoon. He'd read it in the paper. So had know-it-all Gordon Barraclough.

'Yeah, I read that, too. They're being switched on by a mystery celebrity.' Ooh, a mystery celebrity. Who was it going to be?

'A mystery celebrity? Do you know who it is?'

Gordon looked at me as though I'd asked him what two and two came to.

'Course I don't know who it is. Nobody knows who it is, otherwise it wouldn't be a mystery, would it?'

He was right there.

'Well, somebody must know who it is, because somebody must've asked him in the first place, mustn't they?'

Gordon gave me another of his looks.

'The Lord Mayor knows. Of course he knows, but if *you* want to find out, you have to go and watch the lights being switched on, don't you?'

Tony said he fancied doing that. I did as well, as long as I wasn't too late home for my mum.

'Yeah, it'll be good, but I'll have to be home by half past five, before my mum gets back from work.'

When we got to Bankfield Top, Melrose told us we had three minutes to get changed. Everybody ran to the temporary changing room. It's always been called the 'temporary changing room' ever since anyone can remember. We're supposed to be getting a proper place some time with hot and cold showers and things, but I don't reckon we ever will.

The temporary changing room's just a shed. It's got one shower that just runs cold water, but even that doesn't work properly. I started getting into my football togs. I tried to make the shorts as short as I could by turning the waistband over a few times, but they still came down to my knees. And the boots were great big heavy things. Not like Gordon Barraclough's Bobby Charlton ones. I could've worn mine on either foot and it wouldn't have made any difference.

Gordon was changed first, and started jumping up and down and doing all sorts of exercises. He even had a Manchester United tracksuit top on.

'Come on, Gordon Banks, get out on to the park.'

Get out on to the park! Just because his dad took him over to see Manchester United every other Saturday, he thought he knew it all.

The next hour and a half was the same as usual – rotten. Gordon and Curly Emmott picked sides – as usual. I went in goal – as usual. I nearly froze to death – as usual, and I let in fifteen goals – as usual. Most of the time all you could hear was Melrose shouting: 'Well done, Gordon', 'Go round him, Gordon', 'Good deception, Gordon', 'Give it to Gordon', 'Shoot, Gordon', 'Hard luck, Gordon'.

Ugh! Mind you, he did play well, did Gordon. He's the best player in our year. At least today I wasn't on his side so I didn't have him shouting at me all the time, just scoring against me! I thought Melrose was never going to blow the final whistle. When he did, we all trudged back to the temporary changing room. Even on the way back Gordon was jumping up and down and doing all sorts of funny exercises. He was only showing off to Melrose.

'That's it, Gordon, keep warm. Keep the muscles supple. Well played, lad! We'll see you get a trial for United yet.'

Back in the changing room, Gordon started going on about my football kit. He egged everybody else on.

'Listen, Barraclough, this strip belonged to my uncle, and he scored thousands of goals.'

Gordon just laughed.

'Your uncle? Your auntie more like. You look like a big girl.'

'Listen, Barraclough, you don't know who my uncle is.'

I was sick of Gordon Barraclough. I was sick of his bullying and his shouting, and his crawling round Melrose. And I was sick of him being a good foot-baller.

'My uncle is Bobby Charlton!'

That was the fib.

For a split second I think Gordon believed me, then he burst out laughing. So did everyone else. Even Tony laughed.

'Bobby Charlton – your uncle? You don't expect us to believe that, do you?'

'Believe what you like, it's the truth.'

Of course they didn't believe me. That's why the fib became a lie.

'Cross my heart and hope to die.'

I spat on my left hand. They all went quiet. Gordon put his face close to mine.

'You're a liar.'

I was.

'I'm not. Cross my heart and hope to die.'

I spat on my hand again. If I'd dropped dead on the spot, I wouldn't have been surprised. Thank goodness Melrose came in, and made us hurry on to the bus.

Gordon and me didn't talk to each other much for the rest of the day. All afternoon I could see him looking at me. He was so sure I was a liar, but he just couldn't be certain.

Why had I been so daft as to tell such a stupid lie? Well, it was only a fib really, and at least it shut Gordon Barraclough up for an afternoon.

After school, Tony and me went into town to watch the lights being switched on. Norbert tagged along as well. He'd forgotten all about his trouble with Melrose that morning. He's like that, Norbert. Me, I would've been upset for days.

There was a crowd at the bottom of the Town Hall steps, and we managed to get right to the front. Gordon was there already. Norbert was ready for another fight, but we stopped him. When the Lord Mayor came out we all clapped. He had his chain on, and he made a speech about the Christmas appeal.

Then it came to switching on the lights.

' . . . and as you know, ladies and gentlemen, boys and girls, we always try to get someone special to switch on our Chamber of Commerce Christmas lights, and this year is no exception. Let's give a warm welcome to Mr Bobby Charlton . . .'

I couldn't believe it. I nearly fainted. I couldn't move for a few minutes. Everybody was asking for his autograph. When it was Gordon's turn, I saw him pointing at me. I could feel myself going red. Then, I saw him waving me over. Not Gordon, Bobby Charlton!

I went. Tony and Norbert followed. Gordon was grinning at me.

'You've had it now. You're for it now. I told him you said he's your uncle.'

I looked up at Bobby Charlton. He looked down at me. I could feel my face going even redder. Then suddenly, he winked at me and smiled.

'Hello, son. Aren't you going to say hello to your Uncle Bobby, then?'

I couldn't believe it. Neither could Tony or Norbert. Or Gordon.

'Er . . . hello . . . Uncle . . . er . . . Bobby.'

He ruffled my hair.

'How's your mam?'

'All right.'

He looked at Tony, Norbert and Gordon.

'Are these your mates?'

'These two are.'

I pointed out Tony and Norbert.

'Well, why don't you bring them in for a cup of tea?'

I didn't understand.

'In where?'

'Into the Lord Mayor's Parlour. For tea. Don't you want to come?'

'Yeah, that'd be lovely . . . Uncle Bobby.'

Uncle Bobby! I nearly believed it myself! And I'll never forget the look on Gordon Barraclough's face as Bobby Charlton led Tony, Norbert and me into the Town Hall.

It was ever so posh in the Lord Mayor's Parlour. We had sandwiches without crusts, malt loaf and butterfly cakes. It was smashing. So was Bobby Charlton. I just couldn't believe we were there. Suddenly, Tony kept trying to tell me something, but I didn't want to listen to him. I wanted to listen to Bobby.

'Shurrup, I'm trying to listen to my Uncle Bobby.'

'But do you know what time it is? Six o'clock!'

'Six o'clock! Blimey! I've got to get going. My mum'll kill me.'

I said goodbye to Bobby Charlton.

'Tarah, Uncle Bobby. I've got to go now. Thanks . . .'

He looked at me and smiled.

'Tarah, son. See you again some time.'

When we got outside, Tony and Norbert said it was the best tea they'd ever had.

I ran home as fast as I could. My mum was already in, of course. I was hoping she wouldn't be too worried. Still, I knew everything would be all right once I'd told her I was late because I'd been having tea in the Lord Mayor's Parlour with Bobby Charlton.

'Where've you been? It's gone quarter past six. I've been worried sick.'

'It's all right, Mum. I've been having tea in the Lord Mayor's Parlour with Bobby Charlton . . .'

She gave me such a clout, I thought my head was going to fall off. My mum never believes me, even when I'm telling the truth!

Jake's Big Chance

Steve Attridge

He can't stop me. I'm too quick. Ball at my feet, like it's glued to my boots, like it's a part of my leg. Left, right. Little shimmy. Yes! Past him. Another defender. He's waiting for me to make the first move. Go straight towards him, let him know who's in command here. Make him know I'm going to pass him. Make him lose in his mind first. Come on then, come on. Little dummy with the left foot then, yes! Through his legs and round to the right. I am most definitely a class act. There's the goal. Big strong goalkeeper, trying to read me. Will I try to pass him and tap it in, go for accuracy in either corner or just try and blast it and trust to power?

Options. Decisions.

I have two seconds at most to decide, but I let myself think I have all the time in the world. Moments like this depend on how good you are at deceiving someone, making them think you're going to do one thing, then do another.

I make the thought come into my mind. Shoot to the left. I draw back my right foot. The goalie sees it and dives to the left. I change direction, turn the ball to the right and tap it in the net.

Goal!

Cheers from the supporters. One voice louder than the rest, calling my name, almost irritably, angrily.

'Jake! Jake Stephens!'

Why would they be angry when I've just scored a goal?

'Stephens! Jake Stephens!'

I looked up. It was Basher Briggs, the PE teacher and school team manager. He was looking down at me with that broken-nosed, ratty-eyed, mad look that he gets when he's in a bad mood.

'If you'd pay attention instead of daydreaming you might actually get in the team and not spend your life on the subs bench. Now go and get the oranges. It's nearly half-time. Look sharpish.'

So off I trotted to get the oranges from the hut. I distinctly heard Basher use the words 'soft-headed' and 'twit' as I did so. The trouble is, and I'd never admit this to any of my friends or family, Basher is sort of right. The truth is – I'm not much cop at football.

There. I've admitted it. I love football. I think about it. I watch it. I talk about it. My head is bursting with statistics, especially about Arsenal. My great-grandfather was a famous footballer, though he died long before I was born, so I guess it's sort of in the blood, except that the bit of blood that carried the talent obviously bypassed me. Perhaps someone dropped me on my head when I was a baby or something.

To make up for being a bit useless, I daydream. I imagine I'm as good as my mate Darren White, who plays centre forward. I imagine myself as central defender, but so quick and skilful that after making a spectacular fifty-yard pass that could land on a dime, I suddenly pop up, like a magician, in the opposition area, shimmying and dummying and . . . you see, I'm doing it again. Just imagining—

'Come on, Jake!'

'Get a move on, sub!'

They were all calling for the oranges and I dropped a few in the mud.

We won. Darren scored two goals. One was a spectacular looping ball from outside the penalty area that no one, not even David Seaman, could have stopped. Afterwards Darren and me went for a burger and fries and Coke to celebrate.

'Did you see it?' Darren asked, his eyes all dreamy.

'Yes. Excellent. One of your best goals ever,' I said.

Darren likes flattery. It's probably the key to the success of our friendship. I praise him and he accepts it.

'Don't worry, Jake. You'll probably get a few games this season – with a bit of luck.'

'You really think so?' I asked.

'Sure. Well . . . it's possible. Maybe.'

Very encouraging. Thanks a lot, Darren.

Then he asked if I wanted to go to his house to watch a video, but I lied and said I had to go into town with my mum.

I lied because I've got a secret.

Every evening after school I go to the local college. The students all go home at about five and I arrive at a quarter past. The security there isn't brilliant and I go to the back of the college where there's a running track and beyond that an all-weather astro pitch with a big fence around it. If the students want to play football they have to book the pitch and get the key. Most of the time it's not used, though. My dad says it's because students like to do other things, like going to the pub and watching videos. I may not be a great footballer, but I'm a pretty good climber and once I'm over the fence I have the pitch to myself, and because it's starting to get dark I'm not easily visible. Obviously the floodlights aren't on, but there's just enough lights from the main college building to let me see.

Why do I keep it a secret? Because I get fed up with training at school and having to put up with Basher's little jokes about me all the time. I imagine that if I train by myself every night then sometime it will pay off and maybe I'll get my chance in a real match and everyone will have to eat their words for thinking I'm useless.

I work hard in my secret training sessions: running with the ball, shooting, corners, dribbling around stones I put on the ground. The whole lot. I end up in a mucky sweat and run home imagining that I've really improved.

That night it was perishing cold. I ran around the perimeter to warm up, then started trying some ball control, keeping it in the air with my right foot. Useless. I could manage about three then I'd lose it. All the ball control of a duck with a broken ankle, Basher said once, and I pretended not to hear even though I felt a right doughnut when some of the boys sniggered. Darren didn't laugh. I was glad about that. You need to feel someone's on your side.

I was just practising turning quickly on the ball when I saw him out of the corner of my eye. I assumed it was a him. A shadow. In one of the corners. A security guard? He wasn't a big bloke, so maybe not.

I didn't feel frightened. I knew that if it was some nutter I could run for the fence and be over it in a flash. But what worried me was – how did he get in? The gate was padlocked. The only way in was over the fence and if someone had climbed over a three-metre fence surely I would have seen them.

'Don't panic, don't panic,' I whispered to myself. I slowly dribbled the ball away to the opposite corner, planning to get as far away as possible from him, then get over the fence and leg it. When I reached the corner I turned to look. He had gone. Vanished.

Maybe I had got it wrong and there had been no one there at all. In any case, I soon forgot about it and went home.

That night I had an amazing dream in which I was given a regular place as central defender and people called me 'The Rock' because I was so solid at the back. Being a modest lad, I merely smiled shyly when all my team-mates congratulated me.

The following Saturday was an important game. If we won we'd go third in the local schools league, the highest we'd been for three seasons. Basher was in a real state about it. On Friday after school he was giving his 'fire and guts' talk before announcing the team for the Saturday.

'Fire and guts, that's what I want,' he said, his piercing eyes accusing each of us in turn. 'I want you to win so much that it burns you even to think about it, so when you go out you're more fired up than you've ever been before. And when it gets tough you'll need the guts to hang on until the game turns your way. Remember – no guts, no glory.'

We'd all heard this before. I'd made Darren wet himself laughing one day when I did this daffy, cross-eyed impression of Basher, shouting like I was demented: 'Remember – no guts, no lunch!'

Basher finished his speech and announced the team. I knew I'd be left out, and I was.

'Subs – Graham Mallett, Rameesh Misam, Jake Stephens. And Jake – try to watch the match and not drift off into fairyland.'

'Yes, sir,' I said, as some of the boys sniggered at his unfunny joke.

It was a tense match. The opposition had two good forwards and our defence, never the strongest part of the team, seemed for some of the time to be on a kamikaze mission. Basher nearly had a fit as he ran up and down the touchline shouting.

'Daniel! How many times do I have to tell you? Don't play games in your own penalty box. If in doubt, boot it!'

Daniel Jones looked out to lunch and eventually he failed to clear an easy ball and gave a goal away. At half-time we were one–nil down.

'That was pathetic!' shouted Basher, little flecks of spit on his lips. 'Defenders, they've got a real goal-hanger, so all you need to do is . . . what?'

'Play him offside,' I said without thinking.

'Play him offside,' Basher repeated, then he looked at me. 'Are you being sarcastic, Jake Stephens?'

'No, sir. It's just . . . obvious.'

Basher sneered at me, then continued with his tirade.

During the second half I imagined myself commanding the back four majestically, moving them up to play offside, doing great tackles and playing long passes that Glen Hoddle would applaud. While I was imagining this we went down another two goals and lost the match.

Darren stalked off and wouldn't speak to anyone. Basher looked as if he might suddenly become an axe murderer. No chance of winning the Schools League now. But there was still the cup.

*

That evening I went to the college and climbed over the fence. It was quite dark but there was just enough light to train. After a few aimless kicks I went back over the game we had just lost, imagining what I would have done.

'Here comes the centre forward. I wait for him to commit himself. He goes to my left and I time my tackle perfectly – a wonderful block that takes the ball as his momentum carries him forward. I don't panic, don't rush. Take a moment to look up and get a map of where everyone is. I notice someone on the wing calling and deliver a sweet pass just in front of him. I also notice a gap straight through the middle and set off, attacking space and claiming it. Breathless, but full of purpose. Gaining pace. Looking for the gaps. I'm well in their penalty area and the winger looks up, sees me and aims the long ball. It's coming in high, but I know I won't use my head. I shuffle to the side, bring the ball down on my chest, to the ground and turn it to my best right foot, pull the trigger and—'

Suddenly the floodlights snapped on. I stopped, my breath froze on my lips with fear. It was like bright daylight. Here I was, talking to myself, and I hadn't even noticed anyone approach.

I looked around. In the far corner was a figure wearing a long coat or cloak with the collar turned up.

I decided to leg it. I turned and ran at the fence. I looked up and stopped dead. Now he was there in front of me. How did he get from one corner to another in about three seconds flat? This was weird and I didn't like it. Who was he? What was he?

I turned and started to run towards the far fence but the figure suddenly appeared again. I stopped and listened to my heart thumping like a drum. I'd never been this frightened. He was about ten metres away and I could feel him looking at me, even though I couldn't see.

'Are you the guard?' I asked.

No reply.

'What do you want?'

'I want to ask two questions,' the figure said.

'What?' I asked, curious despite my terror.

'Why didn't you use your head?'

He'd been listening to me. I don't know why, but for some weird reason I decided to tell the truth. Sometimes that's a mistake.

'Because it hurts. I'm a lousy header.'

'Only if you're doing it wrong,' he said.

True enough.

'What's the second question?' I asked.

'You brought the ball down and wasted at least a second putting it on to your right foot. Because you don't trust your left foot to do the job. Am I right?'

'Yes,' I answered.

'I can put that right, my old cocker, if you want,' he said.

I looked at him. He had approached and was standing in the light. He was quite a small man, and wore a sort of trenchcoat so long that I couldn't see his feet. He had quite an old face, nut-brown and wrinkled with crinkle lines at the corners of his eyes, which were small, sharp and blue. What could this funny little old bloke know about football?

He must have read my thoughts because he said, 'More than you think. Well, are you going to stand there all night like a stuffed tater, or do we get to work?'

What did I have to lose? Certainly not a place in the

team. I could humour this oddball for an hour or so and it wouldn't cost me anything.

'All right. You're on,' I said.

He smiled a big cheesy smile and took off his trench-coat. I couldn't stop myself from laughing. He wore baggy white shorts about ten sizes too big that flapped like flags around his skinny little legs. He wore a shirt so ragged and faded that you couldn't tell what the original colours were. Boots that came straight from a museum. I was about to tell him that you couldn't wear boots on an astro pitch, but why bother? He was obviously as nutty as a wasp's nest.

For the next ten minutes he showed me how to head the ball, using the pace of the ball to get power, rather than giving myself concussion. He seemed to know what he was talking about and, for an old bloke, was quite agile. Then he made me use my left foot only with different kinds of kicks: side-foot, inside and outside of the foot; keeping the ball low by crouching over it when you kick. Before I knew it, it was eight o'clock.

'Blimey! I'd better get home quick,' I said.

He smiled. 'Same time next week?' he asked.

'You bet,' I said.

Every night I went and trained on the astro pitch. A week later the old man was there again. He watched what I'd been practising, muttered that it could be better. Then we did passing. We ran along together and he was surprisingly nimble – every pass he made was just far enough in front of me to make me run on to the ball. A lot of my passes missed the mark.

'In front! In front! You mustn't slow the player

down. Make him work. Make him run for it. Make the pass push the game on.'

I passed the ball too far in front. He ran for it, skidded and tumbled over. I heard a crack and ran over to him. He was holding his ankle and wincing in pain.

'Are you all right?' I asked, knowing it was a stupid question.

'Old injury. I got it in . . . never mind. Help me up,' he said.

The training session was over. He hobbled away on his own, even though I offered to go and call an ambulance.

Amazingly, the next week he was back. I didn't understand. I'd heard his ankle go. How could someone, especially someone old, recover from a broken ankle in a week? It wasn't possible, but there he was, with that big cheesy grin again.

'What about the ankle?' I asked.

'Good as new,' he said, keeping the ball in the air with alternating feet.

That evening we worked on penalties. He told me that a penalty was either won or lost before it was even taken. You made up your mind which way to go, then tried to make everything – the look, the run-up – appear as if you were going the other way. The golden rule was: don't change your mind.

I went in goal and he scored six out of six. I tried, with him in goal, and scored two out of six, then three out of the next six, then two again. Lousy average. I kicked the ball away in disgust.

'Never do that! It shows defeat,' he said.

I must admit, I'd had enough. It was the cup match a week on Saturday and I was sub as usual. I hadn't had a full game all season. So what was the use of all this training?

'What do you know anyway?' I snapped as the old man gave me the ball.

If he was hurt, he didn't show it.

'Not much. But I've picked up a few things. Shall we carry on?' he said, handing me the ball.

I took it and threw it down again. I'm like that sometimes. It's pathetic really.

'What's the point? I'm not in the cup team. I can't get the penalties right. All this training and I'm still sub, and still Basher thinks I'm a king nerd.'

'Forget him. Just practise. Your time will come, my old cocker,' he said.

Now the fuse had been lit in me, there was no stopping it. My dad says that sometimes I'm my own worst enemy.

'Oh yeah. And how would some old twit like you know? You got second sight or something?' I shouted, regretting it instantly, but once I'd got my mouth open the words just tumbled out like little demons.

He didn't look at me, didn't even show he'd heard. He just put on his old trenchcoat and walked away. I waited for him to turn back but he didn't.

'See you next Tuesday?' I shouted, but he was gone. Don't ask me where or how. I don't know. He'd just vanished. It wasn't weird or scary. Just lonely. And the floodlights snapped off.

Next Tuesday I waited until gone eight o'clock but he didn't come. Every time I heard a breeze through the wires or saw a shadow flicker outside the fence I thought it might be him, but it never was. I'd blown it. I tried training but my heart wasn't in it. In fact, my heart felt as if it had been a bit kicked around itself, and I had nobody to blame but myself. I prefer it when you can blame someone else, but every time I imagined a finger pointing at the old man it bent right round and aimed at me. If I'd known his name I could have looked him up in the telephone directory, but I didn't. I didn't.

On the Thursday before the match I could hardly believe my luck. Flu was ravaging the school and two of the team, including defender Daniel, were in bed for at least a week. Plus, the two other subs were ill with flu too. *Yes!* I said a small thank-you to the flu bug.

Basher had aged about a hundred years since the epidemic and he looked up greyly from the team sheet as he announced the names. Finally he looked at me.

'Jake Stephens, central defender.'

I never thought I'd hear the words. Darren winked at me and smiled. I wish I could have told the old man but . . .

Basher interrupted my thoughts.

'Jake, you're in the team because there's no one else. Just try not to float off into dreamland. Keep to the basics and try not to make more mistakes than necessary. Got it?'

'Got it, sir,' I said.

Basher certainly knew how to inspire confidence. Even so, I felt as tall as a skyscraper as I walked home.

It's a windy day, a bit cold if you stand around, but I don't intend standing around. There's quite a good crowd – about fifty people, including my mum and dad. Basher is pacing up and down the touchline like a demented cat. I never thought I'd play in a cup match but here I am, thanks to the flu. The other team is from St Joseph's school. I pick out their main striker – he's my man. He's not as tall as me but he looks strong and I notice in the warm-up that he favours his left foot. Darren is captain and he comes up and taps me on the shoulder.

'Good luck, mate,' he says.

I nod. I've got flutters in my belly and already I feel uncoordinated, but in my mind I tell the feeling to go away.

Suddenly the whistle blows and we're off. Nothing fancy. Nothing too clever. Watch my man, make sure he doesn't get too far away from me off the ball. All the play is midfield, then a long ball over. For a second I think I can get to it, but I misjudge the bounce and it's over my head and the striker is away.

I turn and race after him. He's one of those who puts his head down and goes straight for goal. I gain a few inches on him. He's just inside the penalty area and he looks up, ready to shoot. I know he'll try to turn it on to his left foot. It slows him down and gives me that extra second to catch up and slide tackle.

I take the ball neatly away from him and it runs to our left defender who boots it clear. I hear a few cheers and recognize my dad's voice.

'Well done, Jake. Great tackle.'

I've done it! I actually made a great tackle in a real match.

Just before half-time – the nightmare. I'm doing well. Keeping things steady, then I look and realize the other back three have moved forward to play the opposition striker offside. He's waiting for another long ball. I run to join my team-mates, but it's too late and I've played him onside. I race after him but this time he makes no mistake. The ball flies past our keeper.

One–nil. I wish the earth would swallow me up.

The whistle blows for half-time. Fool! Stupid clod-hopping fool!

Basher is not pleased.

'Jake Stephens, do you realize which side you're meant to be playing on? Do you, lad? Because from where I'm standing it looked as if you weren't sure, so you decided to play a bit on our side and a bit on theirs. You may have lost us this match, but you've sure as Moses lost any chance of a regular place in the team.'

I hate him. I bite back the tears. Darren puts his arm round me as we go back on the pitch.

'Could happen to anyone. You're doing your best,' he says.

'And that's just not good enough, eh?' I say.

'*Your time will come, my old cocker.*'

I look around sharply. Darren is jogging off and anyway it wasn't his voice. The voice sounded as if it was right next to me but . . . the whistle blows and we're off again. I get the ball almost straight away. It's tempting just to boot it. Anything rather than make a mistake. But I make myself look up, get a sense of who is where, then I hear a whisper: '*Make the pass, push the game on.*'

I pull back my right foot and deliver a long searching ball that looks as if it's going nowhere, but our left winger, Jason Richards, sees the gap and makes a run. The ball swings just in front of him and he takes it at the gallop.

We both get a round of applause. If I wasn't so modest I'd say it was a pass of almost superhuman vision.

Fifteen minutes to go and we're still one down. I sense the danger even before I know it. Our keeper is off his line, and one of their forwards delivers a wonderful cross. Their striker is up in a flash and heads it down, but I'm there on the line, anticipating, no time to move to get it on my right foot, so I trust my left, just like he said, and clear the ball thirty yards. I look over and I get a glimpse of my mum and dad beaming with pleasure.

Lost one, saved one, but still one down.

Minutes later I see the gap down the centre and run through it. I get a short pass, and look up. There's Darren with one arm up on the edge of the box. He's just onside. I float a long ball almost perfectly just in front of him. He takes it, beats a defender, runs, then round another defender and scrambles it in through the keeper's legs. Cheeky! One all!

Three minutes to go and the spectators are cheering like their lives depended on it.

'Go, Darren, go!' Basher shouts, his voice all sandpapery from shouting, his face red as a raspberry and just as hairy. Darren makes a last-ditch effort, takes the ball from inside the halfway line and just runs, only the goal on his mind. He beats one player, then gets into the penalty box. A defender crashes in from behind and Darren almost does a double somersault.

Penalty.

Darren usually takes the penalties, but he can only just about stand. We all cluster around Darren. The other striker, Martin Spencer, insists on taking it, but midfield James Watson fancies his chances too. I step forward and take the ball from Darren.

'I'm on for this one. It's mine,' I say, much to my own surprise.

They all look at me, gobsmacked.

'You?' Martin asks. 'But you're only in the team because everyone else has flu. And that first goal was your fault.'

'And since then he's played a blinder, which is more than you have,' says Darren. He looks at me. 'Go for it, Jake.'

When Basher sees me put the ball on the spot he has a fit. I can hear him shouting, 'No! No! Darren! Not Jake!'

Even without looking I'm aware that my mum and dad are glaring daggers at him. I don't care. Basher's voice is a million miles away, in another world. I'm in a penalty world.

I hear him saying, like he's right next to me: '*A penalty is either lost or won before it's even taken.*'

I decide. On the instep and into the right side of the goal. I give a couple of small glances to the left and make sure the keeper sees me do it. I walk back six paces and turn, no hesitation, disguise the run.

'*Don't change your mind.*'

The keeper has gone to the left and I hold my breath after I boot the ball. Maybe I've overestimated and it'll hit the post. I can't bear it. The ball clips the inside of the post and crashes in. The net rattles satisfyingly and I turn to where Mum and Dad are.

He's there, standing next to them, just as I knew he would be. I see the family resemblance. The twinkly eyes, same shaped nose. My great-grandpa.

'I'm sorry,' I whisper to him.

He says nothing. Just gives me that big cheeky, cheesy grin that crinkles his eyes into diamonds.

The team are all over me and by the time I get back to my feet, Mum and Dad are here too.

I look over at the touchline. No one there, except for the faintest outline, the merest glow, and a good feeling that won't ever leave me.

So You Want to be a Hero?

Mick Gowar

'But are you *sure* you can manage?' Mum looked worried. 'I mean – all that games kit, and the cello as well?'

Alan Bottle looked across the kitchen to the pile of luggage beside the back door. He wanted to be able to laugh, to say 'Of course . . .' He wanted to be able to heft it all over his shoulder like Arnold Schwarzenegger and saunter off down the path whistling. But Mum was right; how was he going to get his football kit and the cello and his normal school bag with his homework and his lunch-box onto the bus and all the way to school?

In his excitement to sign up for cello lessons two weeks before, Alan had forgotten that Wednesday was also football night, the night when the school Under 13s played. Not that Alan had ever actually played for the team, but he was the regular third reserve.

Mum turned to Dad. 'What do you think, Trevor? . . . Trevor? . . . *Trevor!*'

Dad put down his morning paper with a weary sigh.

'You fuss too much,' he replied. 'It's up to him to organize his life. He has to learn for himself that he can't do everything.' He disappeared behind the paper again.

'Couldn't you at least give him a lift,' persisted

Mum. 'I mean – just *look* at all the stuff he's got to take.'

Dad reluctantly lowered his paper again, and for the first time that morning looked straight at Alan. 'He hasn't *got* to take any of it,' he said coolly. 'I wouldn't mind if he was a good footballer or a good musician. But he isn't. He's just wasting his time and everybody else's. If he concentrated more on his school work and less on all the other things . . .'

Dad let his sentence die in mid-air, like Alan's hopes that one day he would do something that would impress his father.

'Go and clean your teeth, Alan,' Mum said.

Alan left the kitchen, closing the door behind him so that he wouldn't hear his mother's whispered pleading on his behalf and his father's cold rationality.

'That's the trouble with you,' said Dad, turning round in the driver's seat to watch as Alan shoved the last bag onto the back seat of the car. 'You don't think before you take on all these things.'

Alan got in and fastened his seat belt as Dad backed the car smoothly out of the driveway and accelerated out of the village.

'It's not as if you're *good* at any of it,' said Dad as they sped past the endless flat fields of sugar beet. He sounded genuinely puzzled. 'For instance, why do you bother with football? You haven't been picked for the team all season – so what's the point?'

Alan sat silent as always. It was impossible to explain to Dad. Dad had been captain of his school and college football teams, a county gymnast and a member of the county Colts cricket team. Mr Gates the games teacher and Miss Pine the music teacher both said it was taking part that mattered; trying your best. Dad believed that the only point in doing anything was winning.

'You're just wasting time and energy,' Dad continued. 'You can't spend your whole life messing about. You have to concentrate on what you're good at. Though in your case, that doesn't amount to much . . .'

Alan's thoughts drifted away as Dad warmed to his theme. *Maybe today,* he thought, *I'll play the cello brilliantly. Maybe today I'll be picked for the team and show everyone. Maybe today I'll do something to make Dad say: 'Well, done, son – I'm proud of you!'*

'Who's making that dreadful noise?' asked Miss Pine.

Alan felt his cheeks burning with embarrassment.

'Alan – play D,' said Miss Pine.

Alan drew the bow across the strings. A horrible cacophony came out.

All the other children in the room sniggered.

'No, no, *no!*' groaned Miss Pine. 'Like this . . .' She drew her bow across the string. It made a warm, low note like hot chocolate. 'Now you try, Alan.'

Alan drew his bow across the strings again. It made a harsh grating sound like a porcupine scratching its fleas.

'Have you practised since last week?' asked Miss Pine suspiciously.

'A bit,' admitted Alan.

He could hear again Dad yelling up the stairs: 'For heaven's sake, stop that dreadful noise! It sounds like you're murdering a cat up there!'

Miss Pine sighed. 'I told you all last week. You *must* practise. You can't learn to play by magic! And if you don't want to practise, Alan, there are plenty of others who do.'

She paused to let the message sink in.

'Now, all of you – once more: D . . .'

Right, Bottle, you're playing!'

Alan's heart gave a lurch.

'Sir?'

'I said: You're playing,' Mr Gates the games teacher repeated. 'Paul Stoddart's away, you're the reserve, so you're playing – on the wing. Here's your shirt.'

He flung the blue and white shirt across the changing room. Alan made a grab at it and dropped it on the floor.

'Oh, no! Sir, you can't! You can't play him – he's useless!'

Alan looked up. Lee Spalding, striker of the Under 13s came rushing across the changing room. His normally high-pitched voice was raised even higher in a familiar whine of protest.

Mr Gates closed his eyes. 'Give me patience,' he muttered. Being competitive was important, but Lee took it too far. For Lee, every match was a matter of life and death.

Unfortunately, as Mr Gates knew to his cost, this was how Lee behaved on the field whenever a decision went against the team. Mr Gates had been proud of his record. He'd never had a player sent off from any team he'd managed – until Lee. And Lee had been given two red cards this season for arguing with the referee. If only, thought Mr Gates, he wasn't so talented. If only he hadn't scored 46 goals this season. Mr Gates knew that without Lee, the Under 13s would be bottom of the league. Unfortunately, Lee knew it as well.

'Look, Lee,' said Mr Gates patiently, 'it's the last game of the season, and we're playing Sefton Mallett.' He paused, hoping that the message would get through to Lee. It was a long-established tradition that every season Sefton Mallett turned up and were ritually slaughtered by what looked like a cricket score.

'Alan's turned up to every practice session this season,' Mr Gates continued. 'He deserves a game for that reason alone.'

'But, sir – you can't!' Lee interrupted. 'He's hopeless, sir – you can't play *him*!' His sharp features looked more weasely than ever. He looked and sounded as if he was just about to burst into tears.

'Lee – enough!' Mr Gates raised his voice. 'I run this team, not you! If I say he's playing, then he's playing – understood?'

'But, sir—'

'I said, that's enough, Lee.' Mr Gates turned away and addressed the ten other boys. 'Get changed, all of you. You've only got five minutes before kick-off.'

He turned his back and walked into the tiny private changing room-cum-office and shut the door firmly behind him.

Lee threw one of the boots in his hand across the changing room.

The door to Mr Gates' room was flung open.

'Any more of that, Lee,' he bellowed, 'and *you* won't be playing! We'll go out there with ten men.'

Lee didn't answer. His face was contorted with rage and frustration.

Mr Gates slammed the door to his inner sanctum.

Lee turned on Alan. 'You stay out on the wing, and out of my way – d'yer hear? If you do one thing wrong

– just one – I'll have you. Understood?' His voice was spiteful and menacing. He glared down at Alan. As he turned to go back to his place on the far side of the changing room, Lee collided with the cello which was propped up on the wooden bench next to Alan. The instrument in its black wooden case overbalanced and fell to the floor with a crash.

'Hey!' Alan protested as he lifted up the cello and balanced it against the bench again.

'Just stay out of my way,' spat Lee.

Alan pulled on his right boot and began to lace it up. He felt excited and worried at the same time. This was what he'd wanted all season: a game at last. But Lee had been right; he wasn't any good. That was what Dad said as well.

Maybe, thought Alan, it'll all be different this time. Maybe the excitement of actually playing a match would give strength to his spindly legs. Alan imagined himself running down the wing and firing over a curling cross that twisted out of the goalkeeper's hands and into the net. He imagined Lee apologizing after the game: 'Cor, I never realized you could play like that . . .!'

'What did I tell you?' screamed Lee. 'It's all your fault!'

'I . . . I . . . I . . .' Alan stammered.

Beeeep!

The whistle blew again. 'Stop bickering, you two!' shouted the referee. 'Free kick to Sefton Mallett!'

'It's not fair,' thought Alan. He hadn't *meant* to handle the ball. It had come flying towards his face and he'd instinctively put up his hand to protect himself. It hadn't been a deliberate foul, it was an *accidental handball*. Accidental handball was allowed in all the games on the playground, so why were the rules different here? Anyway, it hadn't been an opposition shot that Alan had handled, it had been a pass from Lee to a player behind Alan which Alan had happened to wander into.

Alan walked back to where Lee was organizing the other players into a defensive wall in front of the goal. Lee turned round. 'I thought I told you,' he snarled. 'Stay out of the way – you've done enough!'

Alan positioned himself a few metres to the left of the wall. He closed his eyes and took a deep breath. It would all be OK. The Sefton Mallett players were no better than he was; they'd be lucky to find a player on their side who could kick the ball as far as the wall, let alone score.

Beeeep!

As Alan expected, the Sefton Mallett forward miscued the ball. It slewed to the right and trickled reluctantly to Alan's feet.

'Now!' yelled Lee, as the wall broke. 'Fast break!' He began scampering upfield, followed by the rest of the players.

Alan stood where he was with the ball at his feet.

'Pass!' screamed Lee. 'To me!'

Alan kicked the ball as hard as he could. It landed in front of the Sefton Mallett forward who seemed as confused as Alan as to what was going on.

Alan and the Sefton Mallett forward just looked at each other.

'Get him!' yelled Ricky, the goalkeeper.

Alan realized that this was his chance to make amends. The Sefton Mallett forward made his move. 'An open goal, and I'm the only one who can stop him,' thought Alan. 'I'll be a hero at last!'

The Sefton Mallett forward crossed the line into the

penalty area as Alan closed in. The forward raised his foot to shoot as Alan lunged at the ball.

Alan heard the crunch a split second before the searing pain shot from his ankle up his leg. The Sefton Mallett forward toppled over and collapsed on top of Alan.

Beeeep!

The pain in his ankle brought tears to Alan's eyes, but even through the pain he knew that he'd stopped a certain goal.

'Penalty!' yelled the referee, pointing at the spot.

The referee ran over to where Alan was lying, gripping his ankle. 'And as for you . . .' said the referee sternly. Alan looked up, and through his tears he saw a yellow card being waggled in front of his nose.

Alan sat in Mr Gates' chair holding a cold, soggy mess of wet paper towel to his ankle.

The door opened, and in came Mr Gates.

'How's it feeling now?'

Alan sniffed and shrugged. The pain was duller, less sharp and more of a nagging ache.

'Can you get your shoe on?'

Slowly, Alan inched on his trainer, biting his lip as the pain bit into his ankle. When the pain had subsided, Alan gingerly tied up the lace. Funny, his right foot seemed to have grown half a size.

'Hmmm,' said Mr Gates. 'I don't think there's anything broken – but you'd better go to the hospital first thing tomorrow and get it X-rayed just to make sure. And I'd better ring your mum or dad and get them to pick you up. It's six o'clock, will anyone be at home?'

Ring up Dad? Oh, no, thought Alan. He'd be annoyed at being disturbed, but worse than that, Alan could just imagine what he'd say when he found out what had happened. No, Alan decided, even if he couldn't do anything else he could show Dad that he could cope. Even when he was injured. Even if he couldn't be a hero, at least he could show he was brave. Dad had always been a great one for being brave, and not crying or complaining when you were hurt.

'That's OK,' said Alan, with a weedy smile. 'I can manage on the bus.'

Mr Gates looked doubtful.

'I'll be fine, thanks, sir,' said Alan.

Alan dragged himself, his cello and his bag up the steps and onto the bus. He hauled the cello into the luggage space beside the door.

'Strewth!' said the bus driver. 'You've got a big fiddle there – bet it ain't easy to get that under your chin!' He laughed heartily. A couple of the passengers nearest to the door smiled.

'Half to Barrington, please,' said Alan, trying to ignore the feeble joke. The pain in his ankle was a lot worse from waiting half an hour for the bus.

'We don't go to Barrington at this time of night,' said the driver, tapping his watch as though Alan might be unfamiliar with the words *time* and *night*. 'You'll have to get off at Oakshott and walk.'

Alan felt a great weary wave of misery sweep through him. Oakshott! That meant a half-mile walk. A half-mile walk with all his gear, and his ankle! He limped to his seat and gazed out into the gloom. It looked as if he had no choice; he would have to ring Dad from Oakshott and ask him for a lift.

Alan sat and watched the darkened fields go past. Now he wasn't standing on it, his ankle felt much better. No, he decided. He wouldn't ring his father after all. He could manage on his own. He'd show Dad how brave he could be. He'd show Dad how he could be independent and tough – all the things that Dad admired.

'Where *have* you been?' demanded Mum. 'We were worried sick. I was just about to ring the police.'

Mum stood to one side as Alan dragged his cello and his bags up the step and through the front door.

Mum noticed Alan's face. It was pale grey, and he was sweating.

'Alan! What's the matter? You look ill.'

'Can I sit down for a bit? I played, but I got hurt . . .'

'Where did you get hurt?' asked Mum.

'My ankle,' replied Alan. 'The right one.'

He limped into the kitchen and flopped down on one of the chairs.

Dad was watching the evening news on TV.

'Trevor, Alan's hurt his leg,' said Mum.

'Mmmm,' grunted Dad, not turning round.

'Take off your shoe,' said Mum.

'Owww!' Alan couldn't help it – unlacing his trainers was agonizing.

'How did you get home?' asked Mum, as she helped Alan off with his sock.

'I got the bus, but it stopped at Oakshott – so I walked the rest of the way.'

'Did you hear that, Trevor – he walked all the way from Oakshott with all his stuff. And this ankle's in a terrible state. I wouldn't be surprised if it was broken!'

Alan's dad turned slowly round to face Alan. Alan waited for the compliments: 'Well done, son . . . You may not be the greatest athlete in the world, but you've got guts . . .'

Dad simply cast his eyes up to the ceiling and sighed. He looked at Alan and shook his head.

'When will he learn?' Dad asked no one in particular. 'When will he ever learn?'

A Quick Game Before School

Dave Calder

When he woke up he had an edgy headache. It was hot and the pollution control unit was creaking as it struggled to filter the smog. At breakfast the soya flakes had been a flavour he didn't like and his younger sister kept kicking his legs under the table. So it was with a sense of relief that he escaped into the screen-room – so much so that he simply sat staring for a few minutes at the blank glassy vidiwall before clicking it on.

He had almost an hour before the screen would automatically switch to the school site and that irritatingly cheerful voice would demand his name and tag-number. There was no way of avoiding it: the communicator implanted behind his ear made sure he heard the bell.

He tapped a key to load his favourite game and the vidiwall rippled into a long view of the Terra West Stadium. Two more taps and he'd zoomed in to field level and the players were in motion, life-sized and close enough to touch. At first he sat and watched the game, almost hypnotized, as the screen moved with the ball. It was wonderful, far more exciting than the starship simulator. The ball swerved and switched from player to player, as if in a gigantic pinball machine, was trapped, flicked away, bounced from a head, a foot, went rocketing towards the goal. Even though he knew the players were only images, individually programmed to respond with their own style and tricks, he still goggled at their control, howled when a favourite lost possession, bounced on the couch till he was dizzy, gasping for breath. And then there was the sheer energy of it all: no one now would be allowed to run around like that, using up so much valuable air.

Only his grandad remembered the real stadium, the noisy crowds. The boy found his stories unimaginable, almost frightening. The thought of so many people waving, cheering, shouting together, was wildly disturbing.

The screen was focused on the game, and although he could sometimes see the stands behind the players, they were blurred, a vague mass of background colour, and the roaring sounded artificial, the constant waves of sound used in so many of these games. It didn't have the urgency, the explosive surge of his own shouts of delight as the small, dark player intercepted a cross in midfield, turned the ball past one opponent, wrong-footed another, swerved past a third, and without pausing to steady himself, sent the ball rocketing into the net.

The door slid open. His mother came in, followed by his little sister.

'Are you all right, Argone? Oh, you're watching that again.'

'Look, Mum, great goal! Look, I'll replay.'

'No, don't bother, I'm busy.'

His sister was standing in front of the screen, pointing. 'Ball!' she cried. 'Ball! Goal!'

His mother smiled at them both. 'Come on, Dira,' she said. 'Leave your brother in peace. School soon.'

But his sister didn't want to go. She started dancing about, kicking and twisting. She made a sudden snatch at the console on his lap but he shoved it behind him. Then she picked up a headset and pulled it on.

'Mum,' moaned Argone, 'she's messing it up.'

His mother stepped forward and lifted the headset smoothly from the girl's head. Unmasked, her small face showed a mixture of pleasure and amazement.

'Goal,' she said, and tried to grab another set. But her mother was too fast and chased her from the room.

For a few moments he was unsettled, annoyed. He put the console back on his lap and stared dreamily at the keys. What a pest she was. But the headset was a good idea. Wearing it, he could be inside the screen, could feel more like he was really there. He'd tried to interest his grandad in wearing one, asked him how it compared to the real thing, but he'd been rather sniffy and said he couldn't take to these contraptions and preferred watching it as if it was the 'telly'. Whatever that had been.

Argone slipped the soft helmet onto his head. His sister had not yet learnt the trick of closing your eyes briefly as you did this, to avoid the impact of the sudden change to virtuality.

The headset was flexible – it adjusted itself to the wearer so that its web of tiny sensors could control movements directly from brain impulses, and so that the microspeakers were positioned to give the best possible wrap-round sound. Only the screen area was firm and stretched almost from ear to ear and from forehead to chin, but it was so light you were hardly aware of it. Most commands were voice-activated, so now as he found himself looking into the net from the goal-line, he simply said 'continue', and the goalkeeper moved to collect the ball. From now on, as the ball moved so he sped with it, ghost-like, a disembodied presence.

He hovered on the centre-line as they kicked off again. Since most people's experience of anything outside their own rooms was through a V-screen, the machines were programmed so that you could not pass through 'solid' objects. This was partly to make things as real as possible and partly to stop cheating in games. So now as he rushed along the wing beside the lean, long-striding forward, he was automatically swerved around players moving in for close tackles and it felt as if he dodged and weaved with the players.

The ball slipped over the touchline and he glided towards both it and the blurred spectators. As he reached the line his view spun, first looking down the length of the line, then facing the pitch from behind the player who had run up to take the throw. For a second he was irritated because he had not seen the crowd, the faces and actions his grandad had talked about, but then the ball was thrown and he floated after it.

A mop-headed player cushioned the ball on his chest, half-turned and began to make ground up the wing. Blocked by a big defender, he stopped suddenly, swerved, accelerated again, stroked the ball away with his right foot just beyond the defender's reach, hurdled the outstretched leg and, with a crisp tap, laid the ball sideways to a moustachioed forward who took the ball on the outside of his foot. The forward feinted to the right of a back then went outside him and flicked the ball as the keeper was coming off the line.

It was a close thing, but the ball hit the post and the keeper dropped on it, rolling the ball to a back who made some distance down the flank then played a diagonal forward ball to a stocky centre-half. Forced sideways by two opponents he curved the ball down the line and neatly into the path of a lanky forward.

Argone was breathless, his heart pounding even though he had hardly moved his body. It was not simply the swiftness of motion, but admiration too. Perhaps what impressed him most was that these players, even though he knew they were merely binary code, were based on real people – real men who once could have actually played like this. What they had really been like, and even what their names had been, was something he could not know. There were numbers on the back of their shirts but his grandad, who said he thought he recognized who some of the players were meant to be, had explained that any names would cost the makers of the game a lot of money, even after all these years. So instead, when you chose the teams from the start-up menu, you selected letters, though there was a help note for each that told you where a player might fit best and what special skills or tricks they had. The list was long and made interesting reading, but Argone had only tried a few combinations, for he had found favourites early on. He would have liked to experiment a bit more during matches, but for some reason you were only allowed to change two players from each side during any one game.

The stocky player who was running forward, pushing the ball smoothly before him, was one of his favourites – not for any fancy tricks but for his sudden exciting bursts of speed where the ball seemed to run just ahead of him like a dog, as if they were trackers hunting the net. But he was in difficulty now, for two opponents had closed in, and although he tried to turn back and twist round them, one managed to hook the ball and chip it away.

I could have done better, thought Argone. *I'll play.*

So far the game had run itself – the players he'd set up yesterday performed as the game's software computed they would. But by selecting Player Identity Mode, Argone could virtually become any player, seeing from their viewpoint and making their movements for them. Of course, he could only be inside one player at a time, although some older boys on the schoolweb boasted of being able to switch identities so quickly that they could become the whole team.

'Menu Set Player Identity Select Eight,' said Argone, and instantly he was looking across the pitch from the viewpoint of the stocky player.

Turn, he thought, and the headset's sensors picked up the message and his view moved till he was facing towards his own goal. Inside an identity, he could no longer float like an all-seeing ghost. In fact, he was no longer sure where the ball actually was. So when the group of players he could see deep in his half split apart and the ball was suddenly lofted towards him, he was so surprised that his jumbled thoughts made him stumble. He pulled himself upright and concentrated on getting to the ball.

It always felt slightly odd to be a simulated person, but Argone was quite used to the sensation for Identity Mode was used in his history and geography classes. It was simply a matter of control and good timing.

He regained his balance and started running, focused on the ball and watching for players in his own colour moving forward in case he wanted to lay the ball off swiftly. He reached the ball just after it bounced and trapped it clumsily on his thigh. But he'd got it, and he turned and started running, pushing the ball just ahead and trying not to think about what might be behind him.

He felt wonderful, unstoppable, but as the goal got closer he saw the backs closing in on him and almost stopped to think. Slowing was a mistake – they were almost blocking him before he'd seen a friendly shirt. In a desperate fumble he shifted feet and managed to clip the ball outside them to a lanky figure who collected it neatly with the inside of his boot, swerved away from his marker and volleyed. The goalkeeper sprang sideways and knocked it awkwardly so it rolled over the line.

A small box appeared at the top of Argone's vision. *Corner Left*, it read, *Blue Team, Number Eight*. It was a moment before he realized that was himself. As he walked towards the corner he had an odd feeling that someone was near him, but all the players he could see were clustering round the goal. When he reached the flag and waited foot on ball, he had the same feeling, but wasn't able to turn towards the crowd to see if anyone was behind him.

He steadied himself, watching the players mill around. 'Far post,' he muttered, stepped back, ran two steps forward and thought, *Lean back! Kick*! He watched the ball swing out high and drop short onto the jostling heads. A defender headed it clear, another volleyed it away, and Argone joined the race back.

As he reached his own half he saw one of his midfielders intercept a pass and lift the ball over the oncoming forwards across to him. He trapped the ball on his chest, turned and hurried off. He could see several defenders ahead, but also one of his own team making a run on their blind side. Argone hoped he could make a good diagonal pass into his team-mate's path. To be really well positioned, he'd first have to get round one player who was approaching him.

The opponent closed on him with sudden speed and jigged in front of him, mirroring his every movement. It was a small, dark player wearing a number 10. Argone shifted the ball from foot to foot, trying to confuse, but this player was wonderfully sure-footed, and he couldn't lose him. Worse still, the number 10 didn't seem to be concentrating – his whole face was grinning, giggling. Argone found it unsettling and hesitated.

As he did so, the player almost skipped forward, kicked the ball from under his feet and ran off. Argone was startled. There was something weird and familiar about the player. Despite the small man's agility, he lost possession almost immediately to a sliding tackle. As the ball shot loose, Argone made a rush and had almost got onto it when a defender ran in across him. Argone went in hard, kicking recklessly, and tripped his opponent.

Everything stopped. He couldn't move. A yellow light was flashing at the top of his vision and a gravelly voice said, 'Rules Enforcement Function. Infringement. Rerun event – Yes, No?' Argone knew only too well what he'd done. 'No,' he said. But he wished he'd turned down the REF before playing. On the full setting the function scanned everything, would pick up anything even slightly dodgy; the slightest tap or a ball one pixel over a line would trigger its sensors. Still, he'd have to leave the game to change the setting, so he'd have to live with that yellow dot.

'Free kick. Red Team. Play,' intoned the REF, and the player he'd tripped jerked upright and swiftly flicked the ball past him. Now the ball zigzagged from one opponent to another and Argone ran back, trying unsuccessfully to mark a tall player who suddenly ran towards midfield, slipped between the backs and might have scored if the over-forceful pass hadn't given the ball to the advancing goalie.

That odd Number 10 was in the penalty box, Argone noticed, doing what seemed to be clumsy forward rolls. Then the small figure started jumping up and down in front of the goalie, arms outstretched as if to catch the ball. The goalie ran sideways and kicked.

Argone turned and ran forwards, twisting to see where the kick would go. He saw the ball loft and drop on the opposite wing, saw it slipped into midfield, passed back, and then moved forward down his wing. He was ready now, he had plenty of space and felt he could make a clear run. A short pass, and another cut round opponents and then the ball was coming through to him. He ran forward to pick up the pass and as he did so the small number 10 also raced towards him, waving and shouting. Again he had the awful feeling that something was mysteriously wrong, for none of the other players made any recognizable sound.

As his mysterious opponent closed in, Argone could definitely hear, 'Me, me, give me, I want ball.' He was confused. Was there a bug in the programme or was he going crazy? He'd got the ball but didn't know what to do. He could see that he'd already missed his chance, that the defence was getting organized, but he couldn't make himself move. He simply couldn't work out what was happening.

Argone was even more startled when the strange player made a sudden lunge downwards, hands out to grab the ball. He shunted it sideways instinctively and the player stumbled and fell – then sat on the ground screaming.

I didn't touch him, thought Argone, expecting the REF to speak. But instead the number 10 suddenly stopped howling and looked away towards the stands. His face became sulky. Then he said, 'Oh, Mum', in Dira's high voice and disappeared.

Argone stood up, furious and speechless. He couldn't even bring himself to kick the ball. Then he ordered, 'Menu. Game. Abandon' in an angry, choked voice and wrenched the headset off. His mother was holding the other headset in her left hand and his howling sister's arm in her right.

Argone opened his mouth, and it was probably a good thing that at that moment the school bell rang in his ear.

Dog Bites Goalie

Michael Hardcastle

The dog really didn't look dangerous. Playful was how Steve might have described it.

The first time he noticed the little black and white terrier it seemed to be having a game with someone. It kept backing away, backing away and then rushing forward as if being tempted by a prize, a sweet perhaps or a tennis ball. Steve couldn't hear any bark, though, which was unusual with dogs that were getting excited.

Although his team, Rooville, were pinning the opposition in their own half of the pitch at that point, Steve daren't risk watching the antics of the dog for too long. But as he patrolled his penalty area he kept shooting glances at it. For some reason he couldn't fathom, it had seized his interest. Even when their goalie brought off a spectacular save and Steve joined in the applause for the skills involved, he still kept an eye on the mongrel.

Then he was distracted by a sudden raid, a solitary striker breaking from the halfway line to try a long-range speculative shot. He'd supposed Steve wasn't concentrating but the Rooville goalkeeper plucked the ball out of the air almost nonchalantly. Afterwards, he remembered showing off a bit by throwing the ball from hand to hand before booting it upfield.

When, moments later, Steve looked round, the dog

was on the pitch. Worse, it was coming straight for him. Steve thought of giving it a pat but swiftly changed his mind. The dog no longer looked friendly.

'Hey, go on, get off!' he ordered.

Pausing, the dog looked up at him, suspecting something.

'Is it his dog?' Steve heard from someone behind his goal. It sounded like a perfectly natural inquiry. In any case, Rooville's supporters weren't renowned for the quality of their wit.

'Go on, get going!' Steve ordered again when the dog remained motionless. He waved his pink and black gloves to encourage a departure.

The dog leapt – leapt and caught its target, its teeth going through the glove like razors.

Pain flared and Steve shook his left hand fiercely. Dog and glove fell away together. Steve's kick was a gut reaction to the injury and the indignity of the attack. It caught the dog under its belly, lifting it high off the ground like a well-struck football. The terrier soared before falling vertically to the turf. It landed without a sound and lay still, stretched out, senseless.

It was the sight of the dog in mid-air that caused the referee to blow his whistle. The referee's first thought (because he caught only a glimpse of the object) was that someone had thrown a missile on to the pitch.

Horrified by what he'd seen, a spectator dashed from behind the goal to tend the animal. Steve, still wringing his damaged hand, was for the moment thinking only of himself. Then, as he watched the spectator, he realized what he'd done. The dog was still motionless as a stone.

His damaged hand thrust into his right armpit in an effort to reduce the pain, Steve, hunched over, went to see for himself. By now another spectator was cradling the animal's head in his arms and urging it to show some life. A middle-aged man in the sort of black cap a foreign seaman might wear looked up as Steve approached.

'Thought your job was to kick the ball, not harmless animals!' he said in a snarl that the terrier might have envied.

'Er, is it your dog?' Steve enquired. His pain was easing a fraction but he wasn't in a mood yet to apologise. In any case, the dog had been the aggressor. It shouldn't have been on the pitch in the first place.

'No, it's not. Don't know whose it is. But it reminds me of that Punch and Judy dog called Toby I used to watch at the seaside as a kid. Always felt sorry for it. Like I feel sorry for this little one after what you did to him.'

By now, most of the rest of the players, the referee and one of the linesmen had gathered round to offer advice or sympathy. Some were not doing much to conceal their amusement. Rooville's coach was rather late in joining them and didn't seem to realize that his goalie really was wounded. His eyes were only for the stricken terrier.

'Look,' said the ref in a reasonable tone, 'I'm sorry about this but you'll have to get this dog off the pitch. You're right on the penalty spot, you know.'

'I'll give you a hand,' volunteered Terry, Rooville's coach. 'When we get over to my kit we'll try the magic sponge on him. Works on most of my players, I can tell you, unless they've broken a leg or something like that.'

'But what about *me*?' demanded Steve, catching hold of Terry.

'This dog's in a *bad* way because of you,' Terry hissed in reply. 'First things first, you know my priorities.'

'But—' Steve was protesting when the referee touched him on the arm and said that he should return between his posts without delay so that the match could be resumed.

Steve was in a dilemma. Rooville were only a goal ahead in this League Cup Final so if he went off for treatment Pine Valley Raiders would throw everything at them, encouraged immensely by facing only a make-shift goalie. Steve knew that none of his team-mates was really capable of taking his place in goal. All the same, he feared the dog's teeth had caused real damage and he needed professional attention. He hadn't dared take off his inner glove to inspect the wound. His undoubted bravery on the pitch didn't extend to examining his own or anyone else's bloody wounds.

It was wholly predictable that with Rooville's concentration broken, Pine Valley should launch a fierce attack the moment they had possession. Their Number 7, displaying previously unseen wizardry on the wing, sent over a looping centre that Steve would have caught and held nine times out of ten. This time he caught it, couldn't hold it under pressure, and dropped to his knees to scramble for it again in very undignified fashion among hacking boots. He suffered another blaze of pain when someone trod on the already injured hand.

This time courage wasn't enough. He needed urgent treatment, as the ref realized, but Terry was nowhere to be seen so it was Pine Valley's physio who came to his aid. 'Treatment room immediately,' he ordered. 'So don't try and be the hero by staying on. This is for your own good, son.'

The rest of the Rooville players weren't sure this wasn't a fiendish move on the part of the opposition to deprive them of the most vital member of their defence; but they didn't protest. They'd seen the expression on the face of their skipper, Martin, when *he* had seen Steve's hand.

Before that moment Martin had thought he might become the stand-in goalie himself but now he ordered Darren to put on Steve's black-and-yellow jersey. Darren was a hard man in any situation so he'd be willing to suffer in the cause of a Rooville victory.

'You're lucky this game's being played at a top club ground that has proper facilities for everything,' remarked the physio, his arm round Steve's shoulders as he guided him from the pitch.

Steve didn't see how good luck could possibly come into it: he'd been injured twice, once by a mad dog, and now he was probably out of the Cup Final for good. Most people were never so unlucky in their entire lives. The physio, Ken, had a word with his own bench before leading Steve down the tunnel towards the dressing rooms but Steve was in too much discomfort to worry about what was said.

'We'll get you on the treatment table right away,' Ken told him. 'I've sent for our doctor. Think you'll need some stitches. Oh, and an anti-tetanus jab. Can't be too careful with these sort of injuries.'

But the treatment table was already occupied. The dog was stretched out on it, full length, being tenderly ministered to by Terry who looked up at them briefly, said, 'Hang on a minute, nearly finished here' – and carried on.

'But I need help,' Steve protested, upset at the presence of the violent black and white dog, even if it was still comatose.

Suddenly the dog, possibly alerted by Steve's voice, struggled to sit up and barked fiercely. Steve, thinking it was preparing to fly at him again, backed away.

'Settle down, son, settle down, you're all right,' Terry said, addressing the dog in the same phrase he used to his players. He glanced across at Steve and grinned. 'You do know dogs are our best friends, don't you? So they deserve proper treatment, too.'

'This one's not *my* best friend, I can tell you,' Steve replied sniffily. 'Couldn't be any man's best friend, in my view. He's *lethal* in the goalmouth.'

'Wish some of our strikers were!' Terry laughed, patting the animal fondly as he completed its treatment. Steve believed it was only because Terry had his hand across its muzzle that the dog wasn't still yapping at him. Steve was sure it looked mad.

'Anyway, perhaps it just doesn't like pink gloves,' Terry went on. 'Can't say I blame it.'

'What?'

'Maybe it thought your pink gloves were tasty meat or something and it just wanted a bit. Dead natural in a dog, that.'

'Well, it's not having *my* hand again, that's for certain.'

'Anybody know whose dog it is?' enquired Terry, still stroking away. Ken shook his head. 'Well, we could put out an appeal for its owner over the loudspeaker. Can't have just come here on its own – though there are some homeless dogs around, I hear.'

'I heard somebody ask if it was mine,' Steve remarked. 'That's the one real laugh of the day. I'd have it put down if it was mine.'

'Now, now, don't be vindictive,' Terry said soothingly. 'Let's have a look at your wound, son.'

Steve held back. 'Aren't you going to wash your hands after holding that dog? It could have every disease under the sun.'

Terry frowned. 'Look, son, don't tell me how to do

my job. I know it a lot better than you do.' All the same, he went across to the sink and washed thoroughly. Ken, who'd been given the dog to hold, now tied it to a drawer handle with a length of twisted bandage. It didn't protest at all but kept its gaze on Steve and its ears laid back.

Rather reluctantly, Steve climbed on to the treatment table, well aware that the dog's eyes never left him. He closed his eyes and submitted to the painful examination of his wounds before the doctor briskly came in, rapidly gave him an injection and then did what had to be done. At least the pain soon disappeared and Steve was able to wonder how long it would be before he could keep goal again. Whatever the outcome of the Cup Final, Rooville had another vital match the following week. As he'd gained his place in the team as a result of another goalkeeper's injury Steve didn't want to lose it for the same reason.

'Only a minute to go and we're still one up,' reported Terry, breaking into his thoughts. 'So you'll probably get a winner's medal, Steve, in spite of missing half the game. Some guys are just *so* lucky.'

Steve gritted his teeth. He couldn't imagine why Terry thought everything had to be a joke. It could only be because he was constantly dealing with other people's pain.

'Right, I think you'll survive, young man,' the doctor told him, indicating that he could get up now. 'Just take things easy and don't try to grab anything, not even a sandwich if you're starving!'

Steve cautiously got to his feet, his glance searching for the dog. It was still there, still watching him, ears still laid back. This time it didn't bark or growl but Steve knew that silence was more ominous than noise sometimes. Terry saw what was happening.

'Come on, you two,' he urged jovially, 'it's time to be best friends. Stupid to be enemies. Look, Steve, just hold out your hand, show there's nothing in it. I'm sure Bonzo will lick it this time. He's *used* to you now.'

'No way!' Steve retorted. 'I'm risking nothing with that, that killer!'

At that moment there was a subdued sound of cheering and they all knew then that Rooville had won the Cup. The excitement in the treatment room aroused the dog and when Steve moved towards the door, which meant passing in front of the dog, it made a sudden dart at him. Hastily, Steve stepped aside, although this time he restrained himself from kicking the creature.

'See, I told you,' he pointed out to Terry, Ken and the doctor. 'He'd've bitten me again if I hadn't got out of his way.'

'Oh, well, I reckon he must be allergic to you,' Terry smiled. 'Pity, because if his owner doesn't come for him, we might be stuck with him for good.'

They were. In spite of further announcements to the crowd, the terrier's owner didn't come forward. He'd either decided to abandon him or feared the consequences of possessing a dog that had publicly savaged an innocent goalkeeper (which was how Steve described the attack). The team couldn't just leave it at the City Ground and nobody, Steve apart, was prepared to take it along to the Lost Dogs' Home and leave it there.

'Too heartless by miles!' insisted Terry, to general sympathy from the rest of the team, and so it was he who gave it a home with his own family and their many animals.

Martin, who revelled in getting publicity for Rooville at any time, wanted to give the story of the homeless dog to a friendly reporter but Steve managed to stifle that idea. 'They'll make a joke about it, about how the rotten dog bit off more than it could chew, or something like that,' he pointed out. 'They'll say I dropped it or it was a goalkeeping error or *anything* that pokes fun at me, us. Don't do it, skipper, for my sake – the *team's* sake.' So, reluctantly, Martin put the phone down.

They called him Toby because some of the players remembered the sympathetic spectator's references to the Punch and Judy dog. Terry brought him to training sessions. Naturally, Steve steered clear of him and Terry was thoughtful enough to keep the terrier away from his goalkeeper, explaining once to the rest of the squad that Steve was definitely 'allergic' to dogs. The players thought that was hilarious and for much of the next hour they produced barks and snarls whenever they were close to Steve; and when he handled the ball they jumped up at him, yapping or snapping their jaws. But, like every other running joke in football teams, they eventually wearied of it and training resumed its normal pattern. With the solitary exception of Steve the players quite took to Toby: they thought, as Darren put it, he was 'quite a spunky dog, scared of nothing, not even big goalies waving pink gloves at him!'

'Well, he brought us luck, no doubt about it,' Martin said. 'As soon as Toby came on the scene, we won the Cup – even won it with a substitute goalie! So he must be on our side.'

'But the dog was the *cause* of us having to use a sub,' replied Steve, hurt that no one remembered that. 'He almost *lost* us the Cup.'

He found he was talking to himself. Everyone else was full of praise for the sharp-toothed terrier and when Darren declared, 'Toby ought to be our official mascot', the response was enthusiastic. Nobody took any notice of Steve's glum expression.

Suggestions for parading him at matches and providing him with special collars and a jacket advertising Rooville FC were bandied about; and Terry, as Toby's official minder, was listened to with exaggerated respect. Steve knew that he wasn't going to be able to escape the tigerish terrier. He glanced in Toby's direction and wasn't surprised to see the dog's ears flatten and his jaw quiver. There were some situations in life where you simply couldn't win.

Toby was introduced to the crowd at Rooville's next home match and drew a smattering of applause. Encouraged by this reception, Terry decided to take him on a circular trip, leading him on a leash round the ground, stopping now and again for the dog to receive friendly pats. It was only when they passed behind Steve's goal that there was a problem. Apprehensively, Steve turned to watch their progress, was spotted (or scented or sensed) by Toby, who then snarled fiercely and tugged desperately at his leash. The spectators behind the goal laughed when Terry jovially explained that the dog was allergic to their goalkeeper, and that Steve seemed just as strong in his dislike of 'this brave little chap!' Because he was keeping a wary eye on the animal Steve almost let in a goal, saving a speculative shot only through the alarmed call of a full-back and his own swift reflexes.

'Er, I'll move on a bit,' Terry said hastily. But before he'd even reached the corner flag Steve, struck by a sudden idea, was calling him back. Reluctantly, and fearing further insults directed at Toby, the Rooville coach returned.

'Listen,' Steve whispered urgently, keeping one eye on the firmly leashed terrier, 'why don't you station yourself behind the *other* goal? Tiger-teeth here just might fancy going for their goalie. Maybe it's *all* goalies, not just me, that he hates. I mean, some dogs can't stand postmen, so maybe this one feels the same about us. Maybe he doesn't like seeing men in gloves. Could be something as daft as that. So . . .'

Terry nodded in wise-man fashion. 'You could have something there, Steve. I can tell you've been giving this bite business some serious thought. Anyway, good thinking. We'll see what happens.'

Steve noted that man and mascot moved at a brisker pace to reach the other end of the pitch. He wondered how Tegworth Rovers' goalkeeper would enjoy the experience that so soon might await him; and he found that when he took his gloves off to exercise his fingers he couldn't stop himself from crossing them. His wound was healing well but he didn't examine it.

Things happened very quickly after that. Moments after reaching the other end Toby, apparently excited by the goalkeeper's antics, started barking very loudly indeed. The goalie, irritated by the noise, turned to try to silence the dog, still, of course, firmly leashed by Terry.

Rooville's skipper, seeing his opponent so completely distracted, fired in a shot from midfield – and saw the ball sail into the unprotected net.

It had worked even better than Steve hoped. Toby had done his worst (well, not exactly his *worst*) brilliantly. As Rooville celebrated, the distraught goalkeeper yelled insults at Toby and even aimed a distant kick at him. By now, though, Terry was hurriedly walking the dog away from the trouble spot. A spectator and Rooville fan, amused by the whole thing, called out to the goalie: 'Given a chance that little mutt'd bite your leg off. You want to be thankful all he did was bark.'

As it turned out, the local newspaper reporter overheard that remark and was sharp enough to include it in his report of the match which Rooville won by that single goal. And the sub-editor, delighted to be able to put up a different headline, billed the story: 'Dog puts bite into Rooville's attack.'

Steve, no longer Toby's only victim, enjoyed that story as much as anyone.

Football Friends

Colin Harrison

His toes had gone a kind of dark purple colour, mixed with some nasty red blotches. They looked very strange, almost funny. But Jamie Laurence didn't feel like laughing. Jamie Laurence felt gutted.

He threw a cushion across the room and glared at his ridiculous toes. And at the shiny white plaster cast wrapped round his foot. His kicking foot, his goal-scoring foot. A month at least, the doctor reckoned, till the plaster could come off. A whole month!

And the final was next Saturday. For the first time since he had been in the Riverside School team, they had qualified for the final of the Shire Under 11s Cup. They would never win now. There just wasn't anybody else who could get the goals like Jamie could, no matter what Ricky Pendleton said. Jamie had kept Ricky out of the team all season because Ricky, for all his talk, couldn't score goals.

'Jamie, did I tell you we've got some people coming this afternoon?' His mum bustled into the room and put a glass of milk next to him. 'What's the cushion doing over there? Don't you want it?'

'I couldn't get comfy.'

She picked it up and shook it. 'Here, sit up, let's get you sorted out.'

'Mu-um! Stop fussing.'

'Now listen, Jamie, it's no good sitting around being

grumpy. You've broken your ankle and you've got to make the best of it.'

'But Mum, it's the final.'

'Final or not, you won't be playing. Now, as I was saying, we've got visitors this afternoon, the family from South Africa I was telling you about. They've got a boy about your age, so you'll have someone to play with. Now, I must get on with lunch.'

'How am I supposed to play anything with this stupid thing on my foot?'

She gave Jamie a 'Why can't you be more sensible?' kind of look. Then she headed for the door, pausing only to add, 'And drink your milk. It's good for the bones.'

Jamie scowled at her, as grumpy as ever. Milk? Yecchhh.

At half past two he heard the doorbell, then strange voices coming from the hall. He scowled, fed up that he would have to spend the afternoon with some sad kid who probably couldn't even speak English properly.

His mother came in, followed by the family from South Africa.

'Jamie, this is Mr and Mrs Kunatsa. Jamie's broken his ankle – he fell out of a tree.'

Jamie winced. How could she? What would people think if they knew he was the type of stupid kid who fell out of trees?

Mr Kunatsa, a tall, thin, dark-skinned man in a rumpled suit, shook Jamie's hand warmly and said something in a funny accent. Jamie said hello, feeling embarrassed.

Then it was Mrs Kunatsa's turn. Her hair was braided into lots of tight little plaits, each with a coloured bead on it. She was wearing so many jumpers that Jamie couldn't tell whether she was thin like her husband or not. She, too, offered her hand.

'Now, Jamie, this is Newmas.' Mum had her hand on the shoulder of a boy with big, dark eyes. He was about the same size as Jamie. 'We'll go and have some tea while you two get to know each other.'

She led the adults out of the room, leaving the boys to eye each other warily. Jamie couldn't think what to say, so he said nothing. Newmas looked around, big eyes taking in the Newcastle United posters, the computer, the stuff piled on all the shelves.

'Er, have you got a computer?' Jamie blurted, eventually.

Newmas shook his head so Jamie tried again. 'Do you like Newcastle? Or what about Man. United?'

This time it worked. These names were famous even in South Africa. Newmas walked over to the poster and pointed. 'Alan Shearer.' His voice was soft but he spoke English well.

Suddenly the boys were looking at each other with interest. Perhaps the afternoon wasn't going to be so bad after all.

They talked about who was going to win the premiership, and Newmas told him about Orlando Pirates, his favourite team at home. The names of the players and the sides were strange to Jamie, but they were talking football and what else really mattered?

Jamie told him all about the final and how he'd have to miss the game because of his stupid ankle. Newmas really seemed to understand. He showed Jamie how to shake hands in a special way, like his friends in South Africa did. With their hands clasped together he said, 'Now we are football friends!'

Jamie smiled. 'Football friends!' he said.

*

Just before five Mum came in. 'Time for Newmas to go. And look at the mess in here!'

The next few minutes were full of cushions being plumped up, games being put away, the visitors all saying goodbye at once, and suddenly Newmas was being hustled out of the door and the fun was over.

From where he sat grumbling on the sofa, Jamie could see part of the driveway. He watched as the Kunatsas followed Mum towards the street, Newmas lagging behind. Jamie didn't want to watch. He was just looking away when a quick movement caught his eye.

Newmas had darted towards an old football at the side of the drive. With an effortless flick the ball was up in the air, to be caught and somehow balanced on his thin shoulder. It rolled down his chest, danced from one knee to the other, and then bounced three times on his head, the last one high in the air. As it came down, Newmas flung himself backwards, legs bicycling up over his head to send the ball rocketing away into the garden. He twisted in the air like a cat to land safely on hands and feet on the grass.

'Newmas, come now!'

The boy darted down the drive and out of sight.

Inside, Jamie's mouth was hanging open. He hadn't seen a kick like that since . . . was it Brazil in the World Cup? Amazing. Slowly, a smile spread across his face and a plan began to form in his mind. Hmmm. Perhaps the championship might be possible after all.

Biting off a chunk of the fish finger, Jamie said, 'Whrrt r'ey doon . . .?'

'Jamie, don't talk with your mouth full. Just finish what you've—'

Swallowing fast, he tried again. 'What are they doing here?'

'Who?'

'Those people, you know, Newmas and them.'

Mum smiled, 'Well, Mr Kunatsa works for the same company as Dad. He's over here on some kind of training scheme. Dad helped to arrange the trip for them. They're staying in Mrs Wilson's holiday cottage at the other end of the village.'

'How long for?'

'About three weeks. Why?'

'We-ell, what if Newmas came to visit my school? We had a girl from Australia last term. I'm sure Mr Tompkins wouldn't mind, and Newmas might like it, and . . .'

'Jamie, what a wonderful idea!' Mum smiled at him. 'I don't know why I never thought of it. I'll go and ring Mr Tompkins right now.'

By Monday it was all arranged. Newmas would start immediately and spend the next two weeks at the school. Mr Tompkins, Jamie's class teacher, didn't mind at all – in fact, he was delighted. The class had a project to do on Africa and having Newmas as a visitor would really bring the topic to life.

The bad news was that Jamie couldn't go back to school yet. 'The doctor said a week at least,' his mother said. 'So you stay here and rest.'

Jamie had groaned. Wednesday was football practice – the last one before the final on Saturday. He had to get to school by then – had to give Newmas a chance to show Mr Ross what he could do with a football.

He spent the next two days racing around the house with his crutch, knocking things off tables, scattering rugs and cushions and making the poor cat's life a misery. He developed a passion for playing the piano loudly, and took to juggling with cricket balls next to the best china display. He told Mum how glad he was that he had a whole week at home.

On Wednesday morning Mum decided that his ankle was probably strong enough to go to school. He was away instantly, down to the corner to wait for the bus. Everyone wanted to sign their name on his plaster. Everyone except Ricky Pendleton, that is. He had just sneered, 'Well, who won't be playing on Saturday, then?'

'What makes you think you're good enough for it?' Jamie replied.

'I'm better than you, anyway. Look at you. You should get together with my sister, she's into hip-hop!'

The bus came then, before the argument could get any worse. Jamie struggled on board, spotted Newmas and sat down next to him.

'I saw you,' Jamie said.

'Saw what?' Newmas looked puzzled.

'I saw you with my football. At my house. When you were going and you started to play with the ball.'

'Oh, that. Yes, I like to play football.'

'So you'll come then. Today, I mean, to the practice.'

'There is football today?' Newmas's eyes lit up.

'Yes. You must come.'

'But I have no boots, no—'

'Don't worry. Look!' Jamie rooted around in his bag. 'I've brought my kit.' He had slipped it into the bottom of his schoolbag when Mum wasn't looking, to avoid awkward questions. He handed a boot to Newmas. 'It should fit. You might as well use it all 'cos I can't play and . . .' His voice faded away.

'There is a problem?' Newmas suddenly looked worried.

Jamie sighed, 'For me. Not for you.' Then he thought of the final, and the chance they now had. He grinned. 'But don't worry. Just come and play.'

'Well, Jamie, we're going to miss you on Saturday.' Mr Ross, wearing his usual blue tracksuit and with a ball tucked under his arm, shook his head as he looked at the crutch and plaster. 'Who's going to get the goals, eh, lad? We can keep them out right enough, but we'll miss you at the front. Anyway, who's this?' He looked at Newmas.

'This is Newmas, sir. He's from South Africa. He's just here for a few weeks, but . . .' Jamie paused. What if he was wrong? What if Newmas wasn't any good after all?

'Aye, lad, what?'

'Well, he can play a bit, sir.'

Mr Ross looked Newmas up and down. Then, without warning, he tossed the football at him. Newmas took it on the chest and in one smooth movement let it drop onto his right foot and flipped it up onto the teacher's head.

Mr Ross didn't say a word. He just walked out onto the pitch and waved Newmas towards the centre where Ricky Pendleton was practising penalties. So far Billy Stubbs, in the box, had saved nearly everything Ricky had fired at him.

'Can you defend a minute, Ricky?' Mr Ross called. 'I want to send in a few crosses.'

As Mr Ross sent a ball swinging in at head height, Ricky closed right up on Newmas, aiming to cut off a possible header. The South African sidestepped and darted forward to intercept the ball. He chested it down, turned, jinked past Ricky and shot it straight past Billy into the net.

Mr Ross sent in another, low and hard. This time Ricky tried to get himself between Newmas and the goal but he was beaten by a sharply angled flick. This time Billy got a hand to it and knocked it onto the post.

A little crowd had gathered by now, standing silently with Jamie. Again Mr Ross sent a high one into the middle and this time Newmas pulled out all the stops. He moved himself into what looked like an impossible shooting position. Then, as Ricky and Billy started to relax, he flung himself backwards into that incredible bicycle kick.

Bang! Straight into the net.

There was a gasp from the watchers and Jamie was grinning so hard it hurt. Then Mr Ross beckoned and they all gathered round him. He put a hand on Newmas' shoulder. 'This is Newmas, everyone. We'll see how he does as a striker now that young Jamie's out of action.'

In all the excitement nobody noticed the ugly glower on Ricky's face as he watched people crowd around Newmas.

By the next day Newmas was the talk of the school. All the boys wanted to ask him questions, or watch as he worked his magic on a football.

And it really did seem like magic. It was as if there was a piece of invisible elastic between him and the ball. He could use his head, his shoulders, his chest, his knees, even his hips. He could control the ball as well with the back of his foot as he could with his toes. And although he could shoot fiercely with his right foot, his left was still as good as anybody else in the school.

At dinner time Mr Ross put the team on the notice

board. There it was in black and white – Newmas Kunatsa in the team. Reserve. Ricky Pendleton.

Yessss! Jamie punched the air in victory. Now they were in with a chance.

Saturday morning was clear and bright and by ten thirty Dad had dropped Jamie at the ground. He sat on a bench watching the teams warm up, feeling a bit worried that Newmas hadn't arrived yet. Everyone else was there, kicking the ball around and looking good in their bright blue strip. At the other end the black and white stripes of the Oakland team looked menacing.

At twenty to eleven Mr Ross came over and asked Jamie if he knew where Newmas might be. Jamie didn't. The teacher shook his head, 'Well, if he doesn't arrive, I'll have to play Ricky.'

Disaster!

Jamie hobbled as fast as he could to the nearest public phone and dialled impatiently. 'Mum, Newmas hasn't turned up and the match is about to start and I don't know where he can be and . . .'

'Slow down, Jamie. Newmas isn't there?' She was so slow it was maddening.

'No. He hasn't come, and Mr Ross is going to play Ricky Pendleton and it's going to be a disaster . . .'

She cut him off. 'How was he getting there?'

'I don't know. I asked him yesterday if he wanted to come with us but he said no. Said he was already getting a lift.'

'Sounds peculiar. I hope he's all right.'

'Mum, you've got to help. Please. Can't you ring them?'

'There's no phone at the cottage. And your Dad's got the car so I can't do much.'

'Please, Mum, can't you go to the cottage and see if they're there.'

'Oh, all right then. I'll walk over and see if anybody's home. It will take a little while. Ring again in about half an hour.'

'Half an hour! But . . .'

'Do you want me to go or not?'

'Yes! Go. Please.'

Jamie hung up and charged back to the pitch to tell Mr Ross, looking around desperately for a glimpse of Newmas. He was still not there and Mr Ross was in no mood to delay. 'Right,' he said. 'I'll play Ricky. There's no telling whether Newmas is going to turn up.'

Jamie went back to the bench and waited miserably as the minutes ticked by. As the teams lined up for the kick-off, Ricky gave him a particularly smug look. Jamie had a sudden feeling that he knew what was was going on. He shouted, 'Where's Newmas, Ricky? What have you done with him?'

'Sit down, Jamie, and don't be ridiculous.' Mr Ross glared at him.

Out on the pitch the game had started. For several minutes both sides played cautiously. Then Oakland won possession near the halfway. A tall, red-haired boy had the ball. He dummied a pass, cut past a Riverside player and suddenly put on a tremendous spurt into the penalty area. Jamie held his breath. There were several other blue shirts in the box, but all the attention was on Red-hair. Nobody had noticed another Oakland player heading for the far post, running like a panther. Red-hair passed. Billy Stubbs saw the danger and scrambled to get there but it was too late. Panther only had to stick out a foot and the ball slid past Billy into the corner of the net.

Jamie howled with frustration. Ten minutes into the match and a goal down already. The whistle blew and Riverside surged forward. Martin Davis made a good run down the wing, beat two Oakland players and put a good ball into the middle. While it was still in the air the whistle blew. Offside. Ricky Pendleton!

Oakland took the free kick but soon lost possession and back came Riverside again. For the next fifteen minutes they did everything right except score. They won possession all over the field, passed well and made one chance after another. But all for nothing. Not a single shot was on target.

Then an Oakland defender made a mistake. He tried to boot the ball clear but mis-kicked it straight to Ricky. The goalkeeper was out of position, no defenders within reach. All Ricky had to do was kick the ball into the wide open goal. He drew back his leg and hammered it up into the air, way above the crossbar. The entire Riverside team groaned together.

Jamie couldn't stand it! Limping as quickly as he could, he went back to the call box.

His mum answered immediately. 'You were right, Jamie! Newmas is there. It seems there's been a mix-up. Newmas was supposed to get a lift with Ricky but they didn't come.'

He was right! 'That was no mix-up, Mum! Ricky did it on purpose so he would get to play . . .'

'Now, Jamie, don't be unfair. I'm sure Ricky wouldn't do such a thing. Anyway, it's too late now. Newmas has missed the game.'

'No!' Jamie shouted desperately, 'He's got to come. He can come on as a substitute! He's got to!'

In her most annoying *'everything is just fine, so let's keep calm'* voice, Mum said, 'Jamie, how can we get him there? I don't have a car. Neither does Mrs

Kunatsa. And there are no more buses until this afternoon.'

The pips sounded in his ear. Feeling completely gutted, Jamie put the receiver down. He heard a cheer and looked up to see Red-Hair with his arms in the air and Billy Stubbs sprawled across the goalmouth. Two–nil.

What was the use? Turning away from the match, Jamie walked past the changing rooms towards the car park. Andy Stubbs, Billy's older brother, had just arrived in his rusty car to see the game. Andy played in goal for the Town side. He'd taught Billy everything he knew and often came to the rec to coach the younger boys. He called out, 'All right then, Jamie?'

This could be his one chance! Jamie jumped at it. 'No, it's not! We're two goals down already and unless we can get Newmas here, we haven't got a hope.' He quickly told Andy the story.

Without hesitation the older boy climbed back in and started the car. 'Come on.'

They got back ten minutes into the second half. Things had got even worse with Oakland scoring a third goal just before the break. The Riverside team had lost heart, and only good luck and some great saves from Billy Stubbs had stopped the blues being five or six down.

Jamie and Newmas went straight to Mr Ross who was not sympathetic. 'What kind of time do you call this, Newmas? The match is nearly over. If you think you're going to get a game now—'

Jamie interrupted him, 'Please, sir, just let him tell you what happened.'

When he had heard the story, Mr Ross looked grim. 'Right,' he said. 'Newmas, you're on.' He began signalling for a substitution while the African boy warmed up. A minute later Newmas was running onto the pitch to a cheer from the Riverside team, while Ricky Pendleton was getting an earful from Mr Ross.

Oakland had a throw-in not far from the Riverside penalty area. Red-hair got the ball, turned and raced for the goal. Once again Panther made his run. This time the defenders were ready for him, but Red-hair was too clever. He side-stepped, made himself room and shot, hard. Billy Stubbs dived sideways and took the ball brilliantly.

'That's my boy!' Andy roared.

Now Billy kicked the ball long to find Martin Davis, who went haring down the wing. Again he beat his man and crossed well, but this time there was a blur of movement in the box and the ball was in the back of the net. Newmas picked himself up, grinning from ear to ear as the Riverside fans cheered from the touchline. Three-one.

Riverside were suddenly looking like a team again. Almost straight from the kick-off, they won possession and the ball was shot forward to find Newmas on the edge of the area. This time he had two defenders marking him. He turned, flicked the ball over their heads, darted between them, got to the ball before it bounced and volleyed it straight past the stunned goalkeeper. Three–two.

Jamie was waving his crutch and yelling in excitement. They could do it. They could win this championship yet!

But they still had a fight on their hands. Oakland were determined to hang on to their lead. They pulled all their players back into defence and Red-hair took on the job of marking Newmas. He was so quick and strong that he managed to stop passes finding the danger man. The Riverside attack was drowning in a sea of striped jerseys and the minutes were ticking away.

Six minutes to go, and Jamie was biting his nails. Riverside had forced a corner and Martin Davis was taking it. He hit it too long, over the heads towards the edge of the area. Newmas darted back towards it, facing the wrong way. The position was impossible – Red-hair let him go.

Newmas did his trick. Feet up, backwards over the head, a flailing boot made contact with the ball and, bang! It was shooting towards the goal. The stunned keeper put up a hand but couldn't control the ball and it fell right at the feet of Jason Thomas who scrambled it into the net.

Mr Ross was shaking Jamie's hand and Andy was yelling. A little cluster of Riverside parents and friends were singing, 'You'll never walk alone'. There was no sign of Ricky Pendleton.

Three all – and three minutes left to play.

With nothing left to lose, Oakland gave it all they had. From the kick-off they swept down the right wing, throwing most of their players forward. The blues cleared, two minutes left. Back came Oakland, down the left this time. A pass to the middle found Red-hair but Jason robbed him. He looked up, saw Newmas deep in the Oakland half, and hoofed the ball to him. Newmas took it and was challenged hard. He managed to keep both his balance and the ball, then jinked inside the last defender and was clear, heading for goal. The keeper came racing out and flung himself desperately at the ball, bringing Newmas down in a flurry of legs.

Penalty.

Jamie could hardly breathe. Newmas placed the ball

and stepped carefully back. Then he ran in and fired the ball straight at the keeper! Not knowing where the ball would go, the keeper had made up his mind to go right. Before Newmas made contact, he was already moving, flinging his body to the side. By the time he realized that the ball was coming straight, it was too late. He couldn't stop himself. He threw up a despairing hand and got a touch on the leather as it whistled into the net. As he hit the ground, he heard the long final blast on the whistle. Four–three. Game over.

Jamie found himself on Mr Ross's shoulders out on the pitch, surrounded by players and parents and friends. Everyone talking at once. Andy heaved Newmas up too and the two boys were suddenly face to face above the crowd. They clasped hands the African way, and Newmas grinned at him. 'Football friends!' he said.

Teamwork

Gus Grenfell

Seven . . . eight . . . nine . . .

'Rob.'

Ten . . . eleven . . .

'Rob!'

Rob tried to get his head under the falling ball, but it was always going to hit the deck before he reached it. Shame. Just one more and he would have equalled his record of twelve headers in a row. He ran his fingers through his unruly mop of fair hair, put his hands on his hips and glared down at the ball as if it should take the blame.

Standing there like that he looked a little younger than his fifteen years, but on the football field he had a way of making bigger players look slow and clumsy. He toed up the ball from the scuffed grass where it had landed and caught it on his left knee, bounced it to his right, then left foot, right foot and up into his hands. He ran into the house.

Mum was busy clearing up. There was a clutter of plates and mugs on the breakfast bar. She scooped them up and carried them to the sink. 'Could you wash these up? There's a love. I'm off out,' she said. She shrugged into her denim jacket, picked up her handbag and unhitched her car keys from the hook on the dresser. 'I'll see you later. Have a good match.'

Typical Mum, always in a hurry, rushing round doing half a dozen jobs at once.

Rob washed the dishes quickly and then got ready to go. He pushed the blue and black strip of Reedley Under 16s into his rucksack and began to lace it up. The familiar feeling of anticipation and excitement was a small pebble in his stomach which would grow in the next two hours until he stepped out on the pitch. Oxton, their opponents, were only two points ahead of them, and third in the league. Crunch game.

He locked the door behind him as he left. It had started to rain, and a stiff breeze blew dead leaves round his ankles. Not ideal conditions for football. He hoped it wouldn't spoil the game.

The ball hung in the air, buoyed up by the blustery wind. Rob backed off as he realised the big number six had mistimed his header. The ball struck the lad's shoulder and bobbled to the ground. Before he could recover, Rob nipped in and swept the ball out to the right where Jason was coming out of defence. Jason was tall and thin, but not as ungainly as he looked. He rode a clumsy challenge from Oxton's central defender, and set off down the wing.

Rob ran upfield, calling for the return. The defender who tackled Jason had moved out of midfield, and cover was late arriving. Jason saw the opportunity, and pushed the ball into space for Rob to run onto. He carried the ball a few metres forward, but two men were converging, trying to close him down.

Options, quickly. He glanced round the field. The obvious move was to pass it out to the left wing. He drew his right foot back and telegraphed the pass.

Sold! One of the defenders veered to his right to intercept the ball that never came. Instead, Rob chipped it forward with the outside of his boot to where he had noticed Ossie, their top scorer, ghosting in behind the defender on the edge of the box. Ossie took it on the turn, shielding it with his body, and smacked it into the top right-hand corner of the net with his left foot as the back clattered into him.

One–nil.

Ten minutes to go. Rob clapped his hands. 'Come on! Keep it tight.'

Ossie came over, grinning all over his face. High fives and a slap on the back. 'Thanks, Rob. I owe you one.' Then back to positions for the restart.

Rob looked at the huddled group of spectators with their raincoats and umbrellas. People's mums and dads. Reedley Under 16s didn't exactly draw the crowds. Ossie's dad was still celebrating the goal. But not his own dad, of course. He'd said he might come, but 'might' meant he wouldn't. 'Yes, definitely' meant maybe. And there was no sign of the scout from City that Andy, the coach, had said would be there. Never mind – at least they were winning.

It was still raining when Rob came out of the club hut, happy with the one–nil, if not the match itself. He looked slightly enviously at his friends getting into their parents' cars, and wondered if he should try and cadge a lift. A man in a cream-coloured trenchcoat was sheltering under the overhanging roof. He saw Rob and came towards him, as though he'd been waiting for him to emerge.

'Rob, isn't it?' he said. 'Rob Emsley?'

'Yes.' Rob was guarded. The man was thick set and middle aged, with greying hair slicked back and thinning on the top. He had his collar turned up against the weather, though his coat wasn't soaked. He obviously hadn't been out in the rain for long.

'I'm Jack Ambler, from City,' he said.

The name rang a bell. Hadn't he been one of the 1969 cup-winning side? Rob suddenly felt shy.

'I . . . I'm sorry. I thought you weren't coming. You've missed the match.'

'I caught the last twenty minutes. Watched it from the car.' He nodded towards a not-so-new BMW parked on the perimeter road that surrounded the pitches. He wouldn't have seen much from there, Rob thought. 'Saw all I needed to,' he said, seeming to tune in to Rob's thoughts. He took a notebook out of his pocket and leafed through it. 'You're fifteen, aren't you?'

'Yes.'

'Can you come to a training session with the Under 16s on Thursday?'

'What, for City?' asked Rob incredulously.

'Who else? You'll be invited for four sessions at first, followed by a game – possibly more, depending how it goes. You'll be alongside lads already on the excellence programme, and one or two newcomers like yourself. What do you say?'

'I . . . I . . . Yes, of course, that's great.'

'Do you know the all-weather pitches at the training ground?'

'Down by the station?'

'That's right. Be there at seven thirty. They'll be expecting you.'

It was difficult to concentrate at school during the next few days. Rob's mind kept wandering to football, wondering how it would be on Thursday. He didn't tell many people about it, just his mates, but somehow it got around. He was standing in the school yard at break, ready to have a kick about, when he heard someone shouting.

'Hey, Emsley!' It was Brian Mason, a boy in the year above. He was more than a head taller than Rob, with short hair like a black toothbrush and a permanent sneer on his lips. They were both on the school team, and Mason played for another local club out of school. Rob didn't like him much. He was a striker – the sort who seemed to think the game revolved round him. Quick to criticize if a pass went astray, but taking all the praise when he scored. Rob tended to keep out of his way as much as he could.

Mason came sauntering across the yard with a bunch of cronies.

'What's this about you getting a trial for City, Emsley?'

Rob didn't like his tone – it made him feel defensive. 'Yeah, what about it?' he said.

Mason turned to his friends and smirked. 'How much did you pay 'em?' His friends laughed dutifully.

Rob felt himself going hot, but he didn't say anything; better not to rise to the bait. He took a step forward, but felt a hand on his shoulder.

'Don't go, Emsley, I haven't finished talking to you yet.' A little crowd was gathering, sensing fun. They probably didn't like Mason either, but if he got the better of Rob they would all join in. 'How did they find you, then? Is your dad on the board?'

Rob looked around. There was no escape. He would have to brave it out. 'They sent a scout to watch me,' he said, looking Mason right in the eye. For a moment Mason was taken aback, then the mocking expression returned.

'A scout? He must have been blind. Or watching a different player. Did you swap shirts after the match?'

'Actually, it was . . .' What was the point? If he told Mason who had come to see him he would only find some other cheap remark to make.

'Come on then, tell us who it was.'

'Get lost, Mason.'

'Ooh! Temper, temper. Wait till you get there, kid, they'll soon sort the men from the boys. You're not the only one. See you there.'

So Mason was going too. To Rob's relief the bell went for the end of break, and everyone started trooping back into school. Mason and his gang trailed behind, doing a mock commentary: ' . . . and the ball is coming to Emsley, and he's missed it! Oh dear, what a mistake . . . What is this man doing on the field? . . . But Mason's there, picks up the ball. He's beaten one man, two, and another . . . on the edge of the area now . . . and he shoots . . . It's there! What a superb goal!' And they ran off down the corridor, arms aloft.

In the event, Thursday evening wasn't the ordeal Rob had thought it might be. Everybody at the club was friendly, and the training routines were strenuous but not daunting. At first he was a bit overawed by the established lads – they seemed to do things quicker and more effectively than he did – but maybe that was just because they knew what to expect. Most of them were older and bigger than him, too, but they'd all been new once. He tried to relax and concentrate on what he was being asked to do.

At one point they were practising corners; balls pumped in to the near post, far post, edge of the area. Rob started off defending; then the groups were switched round and he was attacking. He enjoyed this, particularly high balls he could run on to. He might be smaller that most of them, but he could jump and he had a good sense of timing.

There was a perfect ball coming over to the far post now. Rob timed his run from the edge of the box, his eye on the ball, but trying to keep an awareness of what the defenders were likely to do. He was just about to jump when he felt a push in the back and went sprawling on the ground. It was too early for a proper challenge, and it hadn't come from the defence anyway. He looked around.

'Sorry, Emsley, you were a bit slow.' It was Brian Mason, laughing at him.

The coach glanced across. Had he seen the original incident or just the aftermath? Rob picked himself up and prepared for the next ball.

Twice more Mason found the opportunity to give Rob a sly dig and put him off. There was no point in picking an argument with him. Rob tried not to let it get to him. If he didn't seem to be affected by it, then maybe Mason would stop. But it was a nuisance, having to look over his shoulder to see what Mason was up to. He was glad when they changed groups.

Towards the end of the session a man in a purple shellsuit and a green baseball cap appeared at the side of the pitch. The confident way he walked up and began watching the action made Rob think he must be someone to do with the club at first. Until he opened his mouth.

'Come on, Brian, get stuck in. That's it, lad. Challenge him, Brian, challenge him! Now, use your speed! Leave him for dead!' It was Mason's dad.

At the end, the coach just had time to say, 'Well done, see you next week', before Mason's dad was there at his elbow.

'Hi there! Alan Mason.' He pumped the coach's hand up and down like a piston. 'I'm a business associate of the chairman.' Then, hand on shoulder, he manoeuvred the coach away from the boys and dropped his voice to a confidential tone. Rob could just hear the words 'my lad' about three times before they were out of earshot. He began to understand at least part of the reason why Brian Mason behaved the way he did.

His own father was waiting in the car on the road outside, which he hadn't expected. Suddenly he was glad to have low-profile parents.

'How did it go, then?' his father asked.

'OK. Good, really.'

'Did you score?'

Rob laughed. 'It wasn't a game. It was a training session.'

'What did you do then?'

'Fitness training, skills, tactics, that sort of thing.'

'Sounds a bit dull.'

'It wasn't.'

'Jolly good, then.'

They drove in silence the rest of the way until they drew up outside Rob's house. Dad smiled and clapped him on the shoulder in a slightly over-hearty sort of way. 'I'm glad the football's going well. I'll see you on Saturday?'

'I've got a match in the afternoon.'

'Come for tea, then.'

'All right. Thanks for the lift.' He climbed out of the car and watched his father drive away. To Dad, football was something to fill your leisure moments, keep you off the streets and out of trouble. He was pleased about the trial, of course, but no more so than if, say, Rob had got ten out of ten in a maths test.

*

Week by week Rob felt himself improving, growing more confident, developing his skills. If it wasn't for Brian Mason, everything would have been perfect. He was always looking for ways to 'accidentally' trip him up, push him over, make him look clumsy.

At school, the sneering and snide comments went on every day. Rob tried to ignore them, but it was difficult. If he reacted, though, he could imagine Mason's response. 'It's only a bit of fun. Can't you take a joke?' One thought consoled him; when they were playing in the all-important match against Sunderland Under 16s, they would both have to pull together for the team and support each other. There was no escaping that.

On the day of the match Rob felt the usual mixture of excitement and nervousness, only more so. He tried to tell himself it was just another match, but he couldn't ignore the fact that it was the biggest game of his life so far. Several others were in the same boat, of course, each dealing with it in his own way. Brian Mason had a new pair of boots. Top of the range Adidas Predator, predictably. He was jumping up and down, clattering his studs on the dressing room floor, making sure everyone noticed.

Rob was sitting down, trying to calm himself, trying to get that feeling of quiet determination that helped him at the beginning of a match. He was playing in his usual midfield position, but the coach had told him to move forward when the opportunity presented itself. He hoped it did.

Only a few minutes to go now. Danny, the captain, was having a word with the new lads. He came up to Rob.

'OK, Rob?'

Rob smiled. 'A bit nervous.'

'That'll soon go. Just play your game. You'll be all

right. I'll cover you on those forward runs.' He punched Rob on the arm and moved on.

They were going out now. The big stadium looked deserted but, glancing round, there were far more spectators than came to watch Reedley!

The referee blew for the start and the Sunderland forward tapped the ball back. One of their midfielders ran onto it, held it for a second or two, then lofted it over the advancing City players, hoping to catch the defence napping. It wasn't well judged, and Rob reckoned he could reach it before the wide man coming down Sunderland's left wing. No problem. He chased the ball and collected it with his right foot, transferred it to his left, turned, and with his right again, passed it to Danny coming up the centre. Nothing wrong with that. Good to get an early touch.

He ran forward into space, calling for the return, which Danny lobbed. It arrived at chest height. He let it run down his body onto the ground and tapped it forward. There was a defender coming straight at him down the centre, but there was a track opening up to his right. He could hear Danny calling out behind him, 'Take it on, Rob!'

He accelerated, swerving round the man who had made the wide run and was coming back to midfield, and made his way onto the wing. Would he be able to get a cross in? There was a defender coming to close him down. It was all a matter of speed.

He headed for the corner. It was going to be touch and go. He waited till he was almost to the line before crossing. Too late. The defender was quick and blocked the ball as it left Rob's boot. It ballooned into the air and the Sunderland man nodded it harmlessly into touch.

An eventful start, but, as it happened, Rob's best

chance to make an impact in the half. The opposition took control of midfield, keeping the ball moving between them and coming in quick whenever Rob or his fellow midfielders got the ball and making them hurry their passes. Rob felt they were too close together, getting in each other's way. They needed more width.

Rob knew it was as much his fault as anyone's, but he didn't have many chances to move out himself. Danny was fully committed at the back, dealing with the lively Sunderland attack, and wasn't coming as far upfield as he might have done. The last thing Rob wanted to do was leave a gaping hole for one of their midfielders to exploit if he lost the ball. 'Keep your shape,' the coach had said, but how could you do that and play inventive football?

Rob was glad when the half-time whistle went. No goals. At least they hadn't conceded any. Maybe they could work out some better tactics for the second half.

The coach seemed reasonably happy with the first half, to Rob's surprise. He did mention the lack of width in midfield, and the inaccuracy of some of the passing, but he felt they had defended well. 'I expect they'll come out looking for goals,' he said. 'Keep it organized at the back; midfield drop back to help if necessary, but look for the chance to hit them on the break. Be patient. You're doing OK.' He didn't say much about the attack, except to tell Brian Mason to do more running off the ball and draw defenders. He'd been doing a lot of shouting, but he always seemed to be running after the ball, to little effect that Rob could see.

The coach had been right about the Sunderland attack. They'd obviously been told to get more quickly into the final third and put the defence under more pressure. Unfortunately it worked; twice in ten minutes. The first was from a corner. The goalkeeper came for it but didn't take it cleanly, and in the resulting scramble a Sunderland boot got to it first and prodded it over the line.

Rob felt implicated in the second. It wasn't that he bottled out of the tackle, he even got his foot to the ball, but the striker was big and didn't go down. He recovered sufficiently to stretch out a leg and push the ball to a midfielder who was steaming in from the right, took it to the edge of the box and thumped it low to the keeper's right and in off the post. It was a good goal, but Rob was disappointed. Nobody blamed him, but he felt he should have stopped it.

After that, Sunderland eased off a bit, thinking they had the game wrapped up. And that was when Rob had his best chance. Sunderland were knocking the ball about, keeping possession, when Rob intercepted a sloppy layoff meant for the wing back moving up. He caught the midfield standing square and was through them in a flash, leaving only their centre back with a realistic chance of catching him as he advanced on goal. He took the ball to his left and ran with it. He was faster than the defender, he was going to get round him. He reached the edge of the area, a few metres more . . .

And then he heard a shout on his right: 'Give it here, Emsley!'

In the corner of his eye he could see Brian Mason on the edge of the D with a marker in close attendance. At the same moment he saw a clear shot to the goalkeeper's right, inside the far post. He knew he could do it. Mason shouted again. 'Emsley! Now!' Rob hesitated for a split second and lost the chance. The keeper moved out and had it covered. And the centre back was on him now.

He pushed it into the middle for Mason to run on to. He came blundering in, all arms and legs, got his foot under it and spooned it over the bar.

The coach substituted them both at that point. Rob didn't mind particularly – he'd been told to expect it – but he wished it hadn't been after an incident like that.

It ended two–nil. Rob was a bit disappointed with his performance. He hadn't really shown his skills much. It had been a hard game; very different to playing for Reedley. When he was changed and ready to go, he saw the coach coming towards him.

'Can I have a word?' he said. 'What did you think of it?'

Rob wasn't sure what to say. He shrugged. 'It was hard.'

'Yes. It's a big step up. To be honest, I don't think you're quite ready for it yet. You didn't play badly. You're a good team player, and teamwork's the basis of it, but you need to be a bit more positive, stamp your own mark on the game. Like that goal chance you had. You should have gone for it; I'd have put money on you scoring rather than Mason. I don't want to lose touch with you, – I like your attitude in training, and you've got good skills. Another year and you could make it. Go on playing for your club and we'll keep an eye on you.'

So that was it. Rob felt his bottom lip trembling and bit it hard. He left the changing room quickly, and there were Mum and Dad – together, waiting for him. His spirits lifted a little. They'd both said they would come, but he'd imagined they would be at opposite ends of the ground; they wouldn't even go around together at parents' evenings.

He'd long since given up any thought of them getting together again, but if they could manage to tolerate each other it would make life easier. A bit of teamwork was all that was needed.

Suddenly Rob felt himself fighting back tears. They weren't going to have the opportunity to come and watch him play for City again. Not this season anyway.

But there was always next season. He'd never give up. Somehow, some time, he would make it. And his parents would be there watching him. Together.

Two Good Feet

Alan Durant

The whistle blew with a shrill peep.

'Now listen carefully, boys,' said Mr Donald. He stood with his hands on his hips, one foot resting on a dirty white ball, inspecting the group of boys standing before him. Each was dressed in football kit and most were streaked with mud from the game they had just been playing. They looked back at the school football coach with eager, hopeful eyes, waiting to see if their name would be called.

'Jones. Tockweed. Stewart. McVay.'

As he heard his name, Grant McVay grinned broadly. Then he went and stood beside his best friend, Mark Stewart. The four boys selected were the best football players in their class, along with Hakim Arif, who was off sick that day. Now, as Mr Donald explained, they had a chance of being in the St Martin's Lane School football team for the opening match of the season against Waverley. Most of the team was made up of pupils from the top class, but there was one place vacant on the team sheet: Mr Donald still needed a left wing-back. One of these four boys, he said, would fill the position. To decide which, they would take part in a penalty shoot-out.

'Right, you four. Follow me,' said Mr Donald and he led them towards one of the goals, dribbling the ball in front of him. He placed it on the penalty spot.

'You'll take three penalties each,' he instructed, 'and the one who scores the most times gets to be in the team.' He raised his thick eyebrows. 'It's as simple as that.'

Grant put up his hand. 'Who's going in goal, sir?' he asked.

'Me,' said Mr Donald. Nick Tockweed groaned.

'It's not supposed to be easy, Tockweed,' Mr Donald said sternly. 'It's a test. Now line up in the order I called you and wait for me to blow the whistle.'

Grant watched the teacher walk over and take his place between the posts. He was a big man and he made the goal seem much smaller than when, just a little while earlier, Grant had knocked a couple of shots past Stephen Lewis. Beating Mr Donald, Grant decided, would be a lot harder. He tried to think positively. But as Dan Jones stepped forward, Grant felt his stomach tighten, as it always did when he was nervous. Mr Donald blew his whistle. Dan Jones ran up and kicked the ball into the bottom righ -hand corner of the net.

'One to you,' said Mr Donald. 'Next.'

Nick Tockweed shuffled forward. He hit his shot tamely, straight at Mr Donald, who had no trouble catching the ball.

'You'll have to do better than that, Tockweed,' said the coach. 'Next.'

'Good luck, Mark,' Grant whispered as his friend prepared to take his kick. Mark nodded, but he didn't seem nervous at all. He looked very calm and confident, as he always did. His confidence wasn't misplaced either, because he struck his penalty perfectly – high to Mr Donald's left, just under the crossbar.

'Nice shot, lad,' Mr Donald called. Then he blew his whistle again. It was Grant's turn.

As suddenly as it had seized him, the tension dropped away from Grant as he ran forward towards the penalty spot. Instead, he felt a rush of excitement. Scoring goals was what he did best. He shaped as if to shoot into the right-hand side of the goal but swung his foot round the ball, rifling it low into the left-hand corner, sending Mr Donald the wrong way. He'd scored. Round one was over.

In round two, Grant and Mark were both successful again and this time Nick Tockweed scored too. But Dan Jones put his penalty past the post and then he missed with his last kick as well, blazing his shot wildly over the bar. It seemed as though Nick Tockweed was out of the competition too, when he shot straight at Mr Donald for a second time. But, somehow, the ball slipped through the coach's hands and legs and trickled over the line. He didn't say anything, but he looked very embarrassed. He had no chance at all, though, with the next kick: Mark blasted it into the same spot as his first penalty. It was all down to the last kick. Grant had to score to keep alive the possibility of being in the school football team . . .

Steadying himself, Grant took a deep breath, then trotted forward and rolled the ball quite gently in the direction of the left-hand corner of the goal. This time, Mr Donald went the right way, but he couldn't quite reach the ball. Grant watched with relief as the ball slipped into the net. Then he turned and grinned at his friend, who slapped his hand in a high five.

'Nice one,' Mark said.

With Grant and Mark both scoring three penalties each, the contest had to continue. Nick and Dan were sent back to join the other boys, while Mr Donald explained what he wanted the two friends to do next.

'Right,' he said. 'You're going to take three more penalties. But this time, with your left foot. OK?' The boys nodded. Grant had no real worries about using his left foot. His dad always insisted that Grant and his older brother used whichever foot the ball came to when he was playing with them. It was important to have two good feet, he said. Grant was better with his right foot, but he was quite comfortable kicking with his left. Mark, by contrast, rarely used his left foot for anything but running and standing on. But in a make-or-break situation like this, it would be as much a test of nerve as strength or skill.

'Right, who's going first?' asked Mr Donald breezily. The two boys looked at one another. Grant, fair-haired, freckled, slight; Mark, taller and stockier, his dark curly hair spilling over his forehead.

'I will,' he said.

'Good,' said the coach. 'On the whistle then.' He jogged away to take up his place on the goal-line.

'Good luck again,' said Grant.

'Yeah, you too,' said Mark. Then the whistle blew.

Mark's first penalty grubbed along the turf and was saved easily. Grant's on the other hand slid straight into the bottom right-hand corner of the net: one–nil.

Mark's second shot was better hit than his first, but it went too close to Mr Donald, who pushed the ball away quite comfortably. All Grant had to do was knock his next penalty in and he'd be the winner. It was a good kick too, hit hard and accurately, and once again the goalkeeper moved the wrong way. But to Grant's horror, the ball thumped against the inside of the left-hand post and bounced away along the line and into Mr Donald's arms.

'Unlucky, son,' the coach sympathized. 'Nice try.'

Grant stood where he was for a moment or two, staring at the offending post, unable to believe his misfortune. Then, slowly, he trudged away. There was a new spring in Mark's step as he walked forward and placed the ball on the penalty spot. He could still draw and take the contest further. All was not lost.

His final kick was low and precise, skimming unerringly into the right-hand corner of the net. A cheer went up from the watching boys. The score was one – all with one penalty left to take. Mr Donald blew his whistle.

'Go on, Grant!' somebody cried.

Grant lifted his foot and flicked a pat of mud from his boot, calming himself. As he straightened and prepared to start his run, he was keenly aware of all the eyes watching him. Now he knew how those players must feel in big-match finals when it all came down to penalties and the very last kick. For an instant a tremor of panic passed through him. Then he drew a deep breath, rocked back on his heels and pushed himself forward.

He was never going to miss. The moment he kicked the ball, he knew he'd scored. Mr Donald stuck out an arm, but the ball flashed past as if catapulted and whammed into the back of the net.

He'd won! He was in the team!

While Mr Donald retrieved the ball, Grant stood motionless, basking in his moment of glory. A hand clapped down on his shoulder. It was Mark.

'Well done,' he said generously.

'Thanks,' Grant replied. 'You did well, too,' he added, sensing the disappointment behind his friend's congratulatory smile. 'One of us had to win.'

'Yeah,' Mark agreed. 'I'll have to improve my left foot.'

Mr Donald came up. 'Good shooting, son,' he said to Grant. 'You're now St Martin's Lane's left wing-back. Make sure your kit's clean for Saturday.'

Grant beamed. 'Yes, sir,' he said. 'I will.'

He walked home on air that afternoon and still hadn't come down to earth next morning when he got to school. Getting in the football team was the best thing that had ever happened to him. He couldn't wait for the match against Waverley to begin. At break he purposely walked past the noticeboard outside the staffroom where the football team and its results were always posted. He wanted to see his name written there in black and white: Grant McVay.

And so it was . . . But not where it should have been!

To his bewilderment and then dismay, he took in the fact that his name was not among those listed for the team. His name appeared underneath, next to the word 'reserve'. He scanned the names above again. In the position that should have been his was written 'Hakim Arif'.

He couldn't believe it. After all that had happened the day before – Mr Donald had said himself that he, Grant, was in the team. How could he go back on his word?

He knocked on the staffroom door. Mrs Withers, the teacher of the top class peered out.

'Yes?' she said brusquely.

'I need to speak to Mr Donald,' Grant said.

'Oh, do you?' the teacher said impatiently. 'About what?'

'About the football team,' Grant said, his courage starting to dwindle a little now.

'Oh, football,' said Mrs Withers with a resigned toss of her head. 'Wait there a moment.' She closed the door and went back inside. A few moments later the door opened again and Mr Donald's big frame appeared.

'Oh, McVay,' he said and he looked a little uncomfortable. 'Look, I've had a bit of a rethink. The thing is, Hakim's a big lad, quite a lot bigger than you, and I think he'll be able to hold his own better in the team. Some of the lads we'll be playing against will be pretty big, you know.'

'But I won the penalty contest,' said Grant.

'I know, I know,' said Mr Donald. 'And you did very well. Hakim's pretty useful too, though, and I'd forgotten that he was off sick yesterday, otherwise I'd never have suggested the shoot-out.' He half-smiled. 'You'll still be reserve, so you'll probably get a game sometime,' he added with forced jollity.

To Grant this was no consolation. Walking back to his classroom, he just couldn't believe the unfairness of it all. OK, he was smaller than Hakim and Hakim was a good player, but surely the least the coach could have done was have another penalty shoot-out to decide which of the two should play in the team. For Grant to win his place fair and square and then get dropped without kicking a ball was just too unjust. But what could he do?

The rest of the morning passed in a blur of misery. Grant just wanted to leave, go home, lock himself in his bedroom and bewail the terrible injustice that had been done him.

'Hey, what's the matter, Grant?' said Mark at lunchtime. 'You should be really happy. I would be if I were in your shoes.'

'I don't think so,' said Grant gloomily. Then he filled his friend in on the situation. By the time he'd finished he was close to tears. 'It's just so unfair,' he muttered.

'Yeah, it is,' Mark agreed. 'He shouldn't be allowed to get away with it. You should speak to Miss Hawkes.' Miss Hawkes was a supply teacher who was standing in for their real teacher, Mrs Appleby.

'Miss Hawkes won't be able to do anything,' said Grant pessimistically. Then he sighed deeply. 'I wish Mrs Appleby was here. She'd do something.'

The two boys sat in frowning silence for a minute or so, then Mark said, 'You could go and see Mr Greer.' Mr Greer was the head teacher of St Martin's Lane. He was Scottish and strict and most of the children were scared of him. He was fair, though, everyone knew that.

'I don't know,' said Grant dubiously. He'd only been in the head teacher's room once, when he'd been in a playground scuffle the year before, but it had left a strong impression. Mr Greer had frightened the life out of him. He didn't fancy going back – even if this time he hadn't done anything wrong. He *did* want to be in that football team though . . .

Throughout the afternoon, Grant fell terrible as his courage ebbed and flowed. One instant he was definitely going to see the head teacher after school to plead his case, the next the whole idea seemed ludicrous and much too scary.

When the bell rang for the end of school, his spirits were low. But as he went to get his bag before going home, he recalled how delighted his dad had been when he'd told him the good news the evening before.

'Haven't I always said you need two good feet?' he'd said with real pleasure. Then with a warmth that made

Grant glow, he'd added, 'I'm really proud of you, son.'
The thought of his dad's disappointment was more
difficult to bear even than his own. What was the use
of having two good feet, Grant said to himself now,
if you didn't have guts to go with them?

He stood for an instant outside the head teacher's
door, listening. There was no sound inside. He tapped
timidly, then waited, heart in mouth.

'Come in!' the head teacher's voice barked. Quickly
Grant turned the doorknob, pushed the door and
entered. The room was just as he remembered: the
big desk covered in papers, the cold grey metal filing
cabinets, the single prickly cactus on the window-ledge
– and Mr Greer glaring at him over his glasses like a
judge in a court.

'Well?' said the head teacher sternly. 'Have you a
message for me from Miss Hawkes?'

'A message?' Grant repeated meekly. Then he shook
his head. 'No,' he said. 'I haven't got a message.'

Mr Greer frowned. 'Well, what is it then?' he
demanded. 'I haven't all day.'

At this point Grant almost lost his nerve. Facing
Mr Greer was much more nerve-racking than taking
penalties. But now he'd come this far, he had to speak
up.

'It's about the football team, sir,' he said. Then, halt-
ingly, he started to tell the head teacher what had
happened.

Grant was worried that Mr Greer would stop him
before he got to tell the whole story. But he didn't. He
listened very intently, prompting Grant every now and
then with a question to keep him going. When Grant
finally finished, the head teacher stroked his chin
thoughtfully.

'Well, Grant,' he said, 'I'm glad you came to see me.

You did the right thing.' His mouth widened in a faint, reassuring smile. 'I'll have a talk to Mr Donald and we'll see what can be done. All right?'

Grant nodded. 'Yes, sir. Thank you, sir,' he said happily, as much in relief that his ordeal was over as with pleasure at its outcome.

'Off you go then,' said Mr Greer. 'I'll see you in the morning.'

'Yes sir,' Grant said again. Then he turned and walked out of the room, closing the door carefully behind him.

Despite the setback he'd had that day, Grant felt oddly light-hearted as he made his way home. The fact that he'd had the courage to speak to the head teacher gave him a real sense of satisfaction. He was pleased now that Mrs Appleby wasn't at school, because it had made him stick up for himself, plead his own case, which he knew was a just one.

He said nothing about what had happened, though, to his mum or dad – or even his brother. He was confident that somehow Mr Greer would sort things out.

He still felt confident the next morning, but when he was summoned to the head teacher's office just before break, his confidence started to slip. Mr Greer had seemed sympathetic yesterday but what if he'd changed his mind and taken Mr Donald's side? What if both teachers agreed that Hakim should play? What if . . .

By the time he reached the head teacher's door his mind was full of unpleasant possibilities. They deepened further when he opened the door and found Mr Donald there with Mr Greer. Then, almost at once, there was a knock at the door and, at the head teacher's command, Hakim entered. Grant acknowledged him uneasily. He felt suddenly vulnerable and outnumbered. But Mr Greer gave him a reassuring smile.

'We'll not keep you long, boys,' he said. 'Mr Donald and I have had a chat and we think that you, Grant, have been treated unfairly.' Grant glanced at the football coach who pursed his lips and looked like he wished he were somewhere else. 'So we've come up with a solution which we think is fair both to you and to Hakim.'

He paused for a moment and gave each of the boys a penetrating stare.

'You'll each play one half of the match against Waverley,' he continued, 'and whichever of you performs the best will win a permanent place in the team. Does that seem reasonable to you?' Grant looked across at Hakim, who nodded. He nodded too.

'Yes,' he said. 'Thank you, sir.'

'Good,' said Mr Greer. 'That's settled then. Good luck to you both on Saturday.' His expression became sterner. 'Don't forget, it's the team you're playing for, not yourselves,' he cautioned. 'The team comes first. Isn't that right, Mr Donald?'

'Oh, yes,' said the coach distractedly. Then the two boys were dismissed.

They tossed a coin to decide which half each would play. Hakim won and chose to play the second half. Grant probably would have done the same. But when Saturday morning came, he was pleased to be on the field for the start of the match. He was too excited to wait around on the touchline for half a game. He'd have to do it in the second half, of course, but hopefully, by then, he'd have proved himself and, anyway, he'd still be high on adrenalin from his efforts.

As Grant took his place on the left-hand side of the field, he glanced across at his dad, who was standing only a few metres away on the sidelines. Neither of them said anything, but Grant smiled nervously and his dad stuck up one thumb to wish him luck. Then the whistle blew and Waverley kicked off.

It was several minutes before Grant got his first touch of the ball – and it was a poor one. He miskicked an easy clearance from just outside his penalty area and the ball skewed off his left boot and into touch.

'Come on, Grant,' one of his team-mates urged.

Grant pursed his lips. 'Concentrate,' he told himself. It seemed to work, for from the throw-in he got in a good tackle and pushed the ball infield to St Martin's captain Danny Howe. He, in turn, swept a pass out to the wing, starting a swift attack that earned the team a corner.

A lot of the play in the first half took place on the opposite flank from where Grant was standing. At times he was itching to go across the field in search of the action, but he managed to resist the temptation.

It was a good thing he did, too, for suddenly the ball was humped over the pitch by a Waverley defender straight into the path of one his strikers who had got into a position wide on Grant's wing. At that moment, Grant was the only St Martin's player between the attacker and the goal. If he was beaten, St Martin's would be in real trouble.

But he held his ground, forcing the striker to move away from goal, then slid in to push the ball away from him and out of touch for a throw-in. The ball was cleared and the danger averted.

Not for long, though. In the very next attack, a long

ball down the middle caught the St Martin's central defenders napping and the second Waverley striker raced through to give his side the lead.

Grant's heart sank. This was not at all what he had hoped for.

For the rest of the half, the play was even, with neither side really threatening. Grant got in a few more clean tackles and played a couple of simple passes, but it wasn't until almost half-time that he got the opportunity to run with the ball himself.

Finally, St Martin's mounted an attack down Grant's side of the pitch. As the midfield player inside him received the ball, Grant moved past him on the overlap. Next thing, the ball was at his feet and there was a long swathe of empty space before him. He pushed the ball ahead and sprinted after it.

When, at last, a Waverley defender came across to meet him, Grant checked for an instant then raced forward again. The defender was beaten and Grant flew towards the goal-line. This was the test. The ball was on his left foot. Would he cut back inside and cross with his right, just to be on the safe side, or go for it with his left and get a better angle?

He didn't hesitate. Reaching the byline he swung the ball over with his left foot. It was a fine cross.

Lurking on the far edge of the six-yard-box, Nathan Starkey had a clear header – but, somehow, he missed the target. The ball slid off his head and past the post.

This attack was the last real action of the first half. When the whistle blew, the St Martin's players trudged to the sidelines. Grant's pleasure at the quality of his cross quickly subsided into disappointment now that his part in the game was over. He'd played OK, but hadn't had to do much, apart from that last run. If only that header had gone in . . .

Now he had to look on as Hakim took his place.

It was the longest thirty-five minutes of his life. Standing on the touchline by his dad, he was torn by conflicting emotions. He wanted St Martin's to come back and win the match, but if they played too well then he probably wouldn't get in the team for the next game.

He felt the same tension, too, every time Hakim touched the ball. If Hakim played badly, then it would be good for Grant and his hopes of getting the permanent place in the team, but it would do the St Martin's Lane players no good in their efforts to save this match. And anyway, how could you wish misfortune on someone in your own team – your own class? Grant couldn't. He and Hakim weren't really friends, but they were friendly enough. At a time like this, being a spectator was no fun at all.

He watched in silent torture.

Hakim didn't start the half particularly well. He was big and good in the air, but he didn't have Grant's speed or touch. He gave the ball away a few times with misplaced passes and once or twice he ballooned the ball straight into the crowd.

He did, however, play a part in the St Martin's Lane equalizer – albeit a minor one. It was from his headed clearance that Danny Howe took the ball into the Waverley half and set up a shooting chance for Nathan Starkey. The goalkeeper pushed the ball away, but straight back to Nathan, who headed it into the net.

'Yes!' cried Grant's dad and he turned to Grant, grinning broadly. Grant smiled back, tensely.

'Why couldn't he have done that in the first half when you gave him the chance, eh?' Grant's dad added, echoing Grant's thoughts exactly. Grant just shrugged.

The game went on – and on. It seemed to Grant as if the second half lasted twice as long as the first. He couldn't believe it when he glanced at his dad's watch and saw there were still nearly five minutes to go. When he'd been playing, the time had just flown by.

Waverley mounted an attack and forced a corner. St Martin's Lane cleared the danger. Waverley attacked again. Once more the ball was cleared.

The minutes ticked by.

There were barely two remaining when Hakim received the ball wide on the left, just outside the Waverley penalty box. Nathan Starkey had made a great run and an early cross would have found him unmarked. But Hakim chose instead to come infield so that the ball was on his favoured right foot. Even so, he made a terrible hash of his cross. The ball spun off his foot and straight to a Waverley defender, who should have cleared the ball with ease. But he didn't. Instead, he took a wild swing and sliced the ball over his shoulder. The ball bounced strangely, looping over the advancing goalkeeper and dropping perfectly into the path of Nathan Starkey. An instant later, the ball was nestling in the Waverley net.

This time, Grant's shout was even louder than his dad's, his smile huge and spontaneous. St Martin's Lane had won the match at the last gasp! Grant was thrilled.

When the final whistle blew, though, just moments later, and he watched the St Martin's Lane players walking happily from the field, congratulating one another, he suddenly felt very lonely and left out. He didn't feel like part of the team: the victory was theirs, not his. He stayed where he was on the sidelines, as the others made their way noisily towards the changing rooms.

Then a voice called out to him. 'Grant! Come on!'

It was Danny Howe. He was at the back of the group, waving at Grant and smiling.

Before Grant could move to catch up with his team-mates, he was hailed by another voice. This time it was Mr Donald. He nodded at Grant's dad.

'Good win,' said Grant's dad.

'Yes,' said Mr Donald. He raised his eyebrows. 'A bit too close for comfort though.' He turned to Grant. 'Walk across with me, lad,' he said. 'I've got a couple of things to talk to you about.'

Grant swallowed drily. 'I'll see you when I've got changed, Dad,' he croaked. His heart suddenly seemed to be thumping so hard it was as if someone was kicking a football inside him.

So, this it, he thought as he started walking. *He's going to tell me that Hakim's got the place in the team . . .*

They walked a little way in silence, then, 'You played well,' Grant heard the coach say. 'It's good to see a young player with two good feet. That left-footed cross you delivered was a beauty. How Nathan failed to score is quite beyond me. Anyway, hopefully it'll be the first of many chances you'll put his way.'

Grant stopped and, for the first time since they'd started walking, he looked at Mr Donald.

'Am I going to play then?' he asked hesitantly.

'I certainly hope so,' said Mr Donald. 'Hakim's not right for that position. Central defence is his best place, I think.'

Grant's whole body seemed to rise. He felt incredibly light and happier than he'd ever been in his whole life. 'Wow, thanks!' he said.

'You deserve to be in,' Mr Donald remarked simply.

He nodded towards the changing rooms. 'You'd better run on and get cleaned up,' he said.

'Yes, sir,' said Grant and he sprinted away across the grass.

He was in the team. He was really in the team! It seemed like he'd been up and down more times than a busy goalkeeper in the last few days, but now, at last, the celebrations could begin!

Terence Blacker
The Transfer

The computer graphic appears on Stanley's screen. A small figure bouncing a tiny white football on his right foot.

His heart thumping, Stanley slips on the headband and places the electrodes against his scalp.

'It works by force of human will,' his mother had said.

The force of Stanley's will is awesome. And he's about to make his wildest, most dangerous dream come true.

Stanley Peterson loves football even more than his computer scientist mother hates it. His obsession takes him on a breathtaking journey into the impossible, where he can become one of the greatest strikers of all time – but where there's a frightening price to pay . . .

George Layton
The Fib *and other stories*

I was sick of Gordon Barraclough. Sick of his bullying. And I was sick of him being a good footballer. 'Listen, Barraclough. My uncle is Bobby Charlton.'

'You're a liar.'

I was. 'I'm not. Cross my heart and hope to die.' I spat on my left hand. If I'd dropped down dead on the spot I wouldn't have been surprised.

Getting into trouble is much easier than getting out of it in George Layton's bestselling collection of funny, bittersweet stories about growing up in the Fifties.

'A rare gift . . . a book whose appeal extends equally to adults.'
Guardian

A selected list of titles
available from Macmillan

The prices shown below are correct at the time of going to press. However, Macmillan Publishers reserve the right to show new retail prices on covers which may differ from those previously advertised.

All Macmillan titles can be ordered at your local bookshop or are available by post from:

**Book Service by Post
PO Box 29, Douglas, Isle of Man IM99 1BQ**

Credit cards accepted. For details:
Telephone: 01624 675137
Fax: 01624 670923
E-mail: bookshop@enterprise.net

Free postage and packing in the UK.
Overseas customers: add £1 per book (paperback)
and £3 per book (hardback).